Colette

MITSOU

and

MUSIC-HALL SIDELIGHTS

Farrar, Straus and Giroux

New York

CONTENTS

MITSOU

Translated by
RAYMOND POSTGATE

*D*ATE: May, during the first Great War. The "Empyrée" in Montmartre is putting on its great Springtime Revue, *Hips and Haws,* and for that it has taken on eighteen young women, one young compère guaranteed unfit "through chest trouble", and a tragedy-actor aged eighty, for the indispensable parts of "Old Man Victory", "A Soldier of Napoleon" and "Marshal Joffre".

The dressing-room of Miss Mitsou, the star. Wall-paper: an imitation pink-and-white *toile de Jouy*; that is, when it *was* pink and white. Mitsou never knew those days. A sort of trestle for a table, covered with face-towels. Wash-stand, a maid's basin and jug. Face-powder in cardboard containers. A ring, with a very fine diamond, in among the eyebrow pencils and boxes of rouge. A small divan about as soft as a park bench; two cane chairs, painted. A general air of "that'll do, anyway".

Time: The interval. Mitsou is resting, alone. She is wearing strawberry coloured stockings sewn on to her tights by the tops, a pair of gilt shoes and a mauve crepon kimono. Nature has given Mitsou all the advantages that fashion is demanding: very small nose, large eyes as black as her hair, round cheeks, a small, sulky, fresh mouth—that is her face. For the figure what is required is a slender body with long and well-shaped legs, and small and low-slung breasts; well, she has all that with only the small defect of a slight skinniness above the knee. But the thirties will fill up those page-boy's thighs, and also the back that is like an anaemic nymph's; Mitsou is only twenty-four.

Mitsou is alone, sitting at her dressing table. Her legs, opened in a V, are held stiff so as not to strain the stockings, but her young back bends and her neck falls forward, as if she were a thirsty gazelle. Motionless, Mitsou would hardly seem to be alive, if she didn't occasionally powder her cheeks, paint red on her mouth, and pick out the corner of her eye with a pencil. The busy hand is not thinking of anything, nor are the big, dark, shining eyes, nor is the melancholy, peaceful face.

A noise in the corridor, a limping step. A knock on the door by an old, dry hand. Boudou, the call-boy.

BOUDOU (*half-opening the door. He is seventy-two and looks older*): Interval's over. You're on soon, Miss Mitsou.

MITSOU (*coming to, slowly*): Thank you, Boudou. Is your foot better?

BOUDOU: Not much better. If there's no change by Thursday, I'll wash 'um and I'll put on a woollen sock and a cotton sock on top of it. Try anything once; that's my motto.

He goes away, leaving the door half open. A noise of soft shoes in the corridor. In the half-light there passes Beautey, the eighty-year-old actor. He stops for a moment, and the light-bulb in the dressing-room shows up the gorgeous uniform of the Imperial Guard, and also Beautey's blood-shot eyes and his disgusting blubber-lip.

BEAUTEY (*to Mitsou*): Everything all right, m'dear?

MITSOU (*hurriedly looking closely into her mirror*): Yes, yes, Mr. Beautey; thank you so much. . . . Oh dear, I am going to be late.

BEAUTEY: Would you like me to help you?

MITSOU (*scared*): No, no, Mr. Beautey; don't trouble. . . . What a thing to suggest!

(*He goes out.*)

MITSOU (*shuddering*): I'd rather die than look straight at him. People as old as that shouldn't be allowed about. It isn't really decent. And I'm so sensitive I even can't bear to look when a horse falls down in the street.

A noise in the corridor of ten small wooden heels. The Five Tireliri Girls run by in a very pleasant English rout. Mitsou is blasé and doesn't notice. Then there pass, one after the other, "War Bread", "Paper Shortage", "Saccharine", and the young actor with the weak chest. . . . There enters an Old Lady in wooden shoes, with a decoration on her shabby fur tippet; she is the Dresser.

Finally, a noise, and with it a series of squeaks like a nest of mice disturbed; and into the dressing-room bursts Bit-of-Fluff. Is Bit-of-Fluff plain or pretty? A good figure or not? She is a scrap of woman whose incessant and intentional writhing prevents you making any judgment on things like that. Dyed hair in a cloud comes almost down to her nose, which anyway turns up to meet it. Mascara'd lashes, clown's cheekbones, the corners of her mouth—they all turn up, as if they had been blown by a gust of wind. Her shoulders quiver, her bottom dances, her hands grasp her breasts (to hold them or to call attention to them?) and if her knees rub against each other, is it because Fluff is cold? or is playing for a laugh? or is just knock-kneed? No way of telling. If Fluff were to fall in the Seine, her closest friends couldn't identify her in the morgue. For nobody has ever really seen her.

BIT-OF-FLUFF (*dressed in a grubby dressing-gown and with a symbolical banana in painted cardboard as a hat; she throws herself at Mitsou*): Mitsou! Mitsou! Hide them for me. Do. They're going to chuck them out and I'll be fined.

MITSOU (*quietly, eyebrows raised*): Who? They?

FLUFF: The two nice boys there, and they're so good-looking (*pointing to the corridor*). Hide them for me, just until Boudou has finished his round. (*Wheedling, and twisting herself grotesquely.*) They won't make any trouble about them being here. You're the star. You can have anyone you like in.

MITSOU (*regally*): It'd hardly be worth while being a star, if you couldn't have guests. But I don't have people in here, and I don't want the company of people whom I haven't met.

FLUFF (*urgently*): Just for a minute only, Mitsou. In your great wardrobe. They're so handsome. (*Without waiting for an answer, she calls in a low voice into the corridor.*) Here, you two, come quickly! At the double!

She brings into the dressing-room two young second-lieutenants, one in khaki and one in sky-blue. The khaki one is good-looking, the blue is better looking.

MITSOU (*looking at them as if they were two chairs*): All this is nothing to do with me.

KHAKI LIEUTENANT: Miss Mitsou, we admired your act enormously in the first part. May I introduce . . .

MITSOU (*apparently not hearing, speaking to Fluff over Khaki Lieutenant's head*): You must understand that if it came into my gentleman friend's head to visit here, before my number Two, with his party that he's got a box for—well, there'd be a very pleasant scene for me in my dressing-room.

BLUE LIEUTENANT (*annoyed at being ignored*): Miss Mitsou, I will not inflict on you any longer a company that . . .

MITSOU (*continuing to speak to Fluff in the same tone*): You must understand too, that so far as I'm concerned I don't care at all whether they're in my wardrobe or where they are. That's not the question. It's just the way things will look. You know I'm not the sort of girl . . .

FLUFF (*overwhelmingly*): I do, darling; I do, I do! But you will do it for me! You are always so sweet. (*To the lieutenants*) Jump to it, you! Into the wardrobe. (*To Mitsou*) The house is full of things; do you know Boudou found one of last year's call-up in the hanging cupboard of that great cow Weiss? He says he's going to tell the management. Old Boudou is a regular stomach-ache. . . .

BOUDOU (*half-opening the door, helpful but suspicious*): You're on in five minutes, Miss Mitsou. (*He looks fixedly at Fluff, who has shut the wardrobe door on the lieutenants.*)

FLUFF (*friendlily*): How are you, Boudou? How's the foot?

BOUDOU (*coldly*): So-so. . . . If it isn't better on Thursday I shall wash 'um, and then I shall put on a cotton sock *and* a woollen sock.

FLUFF: Great sufferings call for heroic remedies, Boudou.

He goes out. Fluff opens the wardrobe. The two prisoners, obediently in position flat against the back of it, wouldn't give up their place for the D.S.O.

They are highly entertained and say nothing at all.

FLUFF: Well! He'd have caught you all right but for
me. The old snooper. I'm on, I'm on! I can hear
the finale of "Poisons of Hell". I must run—stay
where you are—I'll be back. (*She kisses them both
with fantastic speed and skill. In a low voice, to Blue
Lieutenant, pointing at Mitsou*) Don't rely much on
her to keep the conversation going. . . . (*She runs
out squealing.*) Be good, darlings! You're in refined
company now.

This Parthian flattery gets a condescending smile
out of Mitsou. Left alone with the two young men,
who are still upright and still inside the wardrobe,
Mitsou throws off her kimono, which leaves her
clothed in tights attached to long strawberry stockings
and, above, a tulle vest. Calmly, she tightens and ties
at her waist the tape of the tights, opens her thighs to
fix the flap properly, inserts herself carefully into the
red and black froth of tulle which is her costume
("Jacqueminot Rose"), powders her armpits and the
cleavage of her breasts—in short, shows in all her
actions a sullen lack of interest, a careless impropriety
that prevents any thought of coquetry. As she does
this, she thinks it her duty to throw at the lieutenants
the remark: "You all right in the cupboard?" It is as
dry as a biscuit, and it annoys them.

BLUE (*all eyes, but most formal*): Perfectly all right,
Madame, thank you very much.

MITSOU: Oh, now I've become Madame, have I? Talk
of rapid promotion; that's quick enough. (*Silence.
She tries to hook together a belt behind her, and cannot.*)
Where's that old hag Whatshername got to now,
the dresser?

BLUE (*stepping out of the cupboard*): Can I help you,
Madame?

MITSOU: I can't say no. Look, there are four hooks on
the upper part of the leather; I can deal with the
rest; they're press-studs. (*She offers him her bare
back quite coldly.*) Thank you so much.

She says her "Thank you" without turning round to
the picture in her mirror; two young dark heads with
big eyes, that might be brother and sister. Mitsou smiles,
Blue Lieutenant smiles, and they look even more alike.

BLUE LIEUTENANT (*bowing*): Don't mention it, ma'am.
(*He gets back into the wardrobe. A silence.*)

MITSOU (*sits down, points to the divan*): I'm not suggesting
you should sit on that, because as long as Boudou
isn't on stage, you're in danger. As soon as he has
gone down to make the noises off, you can go. It's
Boudou in the wings who makes the Howl of the
Damned, the Infantry Man, and the Flower Pot
that falls out of the Window.

KHAKI (*in order to say something*): A regular Proteus.

MITSOU (*innocently*): No, his name is Old Boudou. It's
always been him, ever since the revue started. (*A
silence. Mitsou is painting her fingernails.*)

BLUE (*civilly*): And are you pleased with the parts you have in the revue, Madame? (*His voice is cold but his eyes are hot. Each time he calls Mitsou "Madame", she raises her well-arched eyebrows.*)

MITSOU: Yes, very pleased. Especially as in this theatre it is not just a matter of talent if you want to be a success.

BLUE AND KHAKI: No? Really?

MITSOU (*importantly*): The difficulty about getting a part here is a matter of age. The management never takes on any girl, not one, who's over twenty-five. It's a house-rule. I'm twenty-four.

BLUE: So am I.

MITSOU: No! Not really? That is funny.

BLUE: Comedy can be found anywhere.

KHAKI: Do you think Miss Fluff is only twenty-five?

MITSOU: So she says. But I expect you know her much better than I do.

KHAKI AND BLUE: No, indeed not.

MITSOU: How on earth's that?

KHAKI (*by himself*): We only met her this evening. One of our friends introduced us and he ran away, the rat, as soon as the trouble started. You know, the 1917 call-up who was caught with Madame Weiss. We never knew the rules were so strict in a café-concert.

MITSOU (*shocked*): This is *not* a café-concert, it is a Music-Hall. Anyway, that's the way things should

be. If there weren't rules, you'd see some goings
on. Now *I'm* allowed to have guests; it's in my
contract.

BLUE: And do you have many guests?

MITSOU (*dignifiedly*): What are you thinking of? Nobody
at all, of course.

As she says this, there is a knock on the door.
Mitsou, startled, half opens her mouth, raises her eyebrows and says nothing. Another knock, and the door
is opened. In comes Mitsou's Gentleman Friend, a
respectable man, in the full bloom of his fifties.

THE RESPECTABLE MAN (*kissing Mitsou's hand*): My
little dear! (*He turns and sees the two lieutenants in the
wardrobe, and gives a small cry*) Oh! (*He is nervous.
Then he pulls himself together and tries to be nonchalant.*)
I told you, my dear, you'd never have room
enough in that wardrobe for all your bits and
pieces.

The two young men come out of the wardrobe.
Their faces show clearly that they hope they're going
to have "some real fun" now.

MITSOU (*unused to emotional dramas, loses her tongue for a
moment; she gets it back only to tell the bare truth. To
the Respectable Man, pointing to the two officers*):
They're not mine; they're Bit-of-Fluff's.

THE RESPECTABLE MAN (*sharply*): Mitsou!

MITSOU: Boudou nabbed them in her dressing-room
and she shoved them in my wardrobe. . . .

BLUE: From which, Madame, we now withdraw, laying at your feet our apologies and our deep respect.

KHAKI (*echoing*): . . . pologies . . . eep respect. . . . (*To the Respectable Man*) Good day, sir.

THE RESPECTABLE MAN (*purple*): Good day. Good day. (*The door closes on the lieutenants. A silence.*) Now, Mitsou.

MITSOU: Now what? (*The Respectable Man stays reproachfully silent.*) Oh, because of *that*! Really, what a thing to fuss over. I've told you; they belong to Fluff. I can't make up stories, I never could. Seeing me look as silly as this you ought to of known I'm telling the truth.

THE RESPECTABLE MAN: Two officers! Two at once! Mitsou, Mitsou, I never suspected you of that particular vice.

MITSOU (*very sad*): Nor did I. Not that vice, nor any other.

THE RESPECTABLE MAN (*touched*): Yes. . . . That's true, Mitsou. But all the same you must admit that appearances are against . . . And they're good-looking too. . . . Especially the one in blue.

MITSOU (*looking up at the mirror which a few minutes ago was reflecting two young faces*): D'you think so?

THE RESPECTABLE MAN: What's his name?

MITSOU (*surprised*): Well, there you are! It's a fact. I don't know their names, or who they are, or anything.

FLUFF (*in the corridor*): Are you in, Mitsou?

MITSOU (*sternly, opening the door*): You'd better come in, anyway.

FLUFF (*out of breath*): Did you send them away? A bit of luck I ran into them. They were going down into the cellars, and . . .

MITSOU: The first thing you've got to do is to apologise to my friend here. He nearly had heart failure. Think of how he felt; coming here and finding two soldiers in my wardrobe!

FLUFF (*nestling up to the Respectable Man, merely out of habit*): Oh, did you *really*, sir? You mustn't be angry with me, please; I am so sorry; and you mustn't be angry with Mitsou either. They were such nice boys. Did you notice them? Especially the one in blue. And his eyes!

THE RESPECTABLE MAN (*jealous*): His eyes? No, not really. Had he a glass eye, or what?

FLUFF (*shocked*): A glass eye! A glass eye! I never saw an eye so . . . so burning with life. And his mouth, did you look at his mouth? Mitsou, did you look at his mouth? And his nose—his beautiful fine nostrils that quivered when he breathed fast! Oh! . . . All the same, now I think of it, Khaki isn't too bad either. He has such a lovely complexion, did you notice?

THE RESPECTABLE MAN (*drily*): I'm afraid I did not give it such careful thought as you did.

FLUFF (*vibrant*): Nothing ever escapes me; it's always

so. Excuse me mentioning it, though, sir; if you don't go now you'll miss the Dance of Moorish Dustmen.

THE RESPECTABLE MAN: I've already seen it.

FLUFF (*all the lady*): Then you will be staying with us? It will be such a pleasure.

THE RESPECTABLE MAN: I'm afraid not. I must go back to my guests. They are two millers, whom I left in my box.

FLUFF: Two millers! Oh. Do introduce them to me, please; are they good-looking?

THE RESPECTABLE MAN: One is my uncle and one is his brother-in-law; they own a flour-mill.

FLUFF (*as if she had been offered medicine*): Pff! A couple of flour-sifters!

(*The Respectable Man goes out.*)

MITSOU (*superiorly*): I hope you have thought of all the trouble you might have caused me this evening, with your army attachments. It's very lucky my friend is a really intelligent man.

FLUFF (*equally superior*): An intelligent man expects his girl some day or other will be unfaithful to him, as she would be to Tom, Dick and Harry. If he doesn't, he's not an intelligent man. And as for trouble—trouble! Life's nothing but trouble!

She throws herself down on the divan, quivering all over, but carefully avoiding rubbing her knees on it, so as to spare her silk stockings.

MITSOU (*pompous and tiresome*): I don't know what trouble is, in that sense, thank goodness. Not for the last three years anyway, since I've gone with Pierre.

FLUFF (*opening her little eyes wide*): No! Go on! I don't believe you. Not even an argument? Not so much as a reconciliation?

MITSOU: Nothing. He never quarrels with me. And I don't pick on him. It's ever so peaceful.

FLUFF: Well. . . . Can't be a great deal of fun, always, the life you lead. And then, what about the front?

MITSOU: The front? What do you mean, the front?

FLUFF (*scandalized*): The front! THE front, Mitsou! Really! There's a war on, haven't you heard? You surely must have someone you're soft on, at the front?

MITSOU: Why, no; I've been going with Pierre since June 1914, you see.

FLUFF (*legs in the air*): What a reason! Oh, well. About those boys, those awfully sweet boys, what part of the front are they in just now?

MITSOU: I don't know.

FLUFF: Didn't you ask them?

MITSOU: No.

FLUFF: Well, what on earth did you talk about?

MITSOU: Oh, I don't know. . . . They asked me if I liked the parts I'd got in the revue.

FLUFF (*jumping up*): About the revue! About the parts
you play! What a thing to talk about to lieutenants
on leave from the front! Where were you dragged
up? Oh God, I haven't got their address! I must
have it. I must have *them*.

She shoots into the corridor like a bullet. The old
Dresser returns; she comes in noiselessly. Mitsou is
daydreaming and doesn't hear her.

OLD WOMAN (*in a faint voice in Mitsou's ears*): They've
reached "Flowers in Prison".

MITSOU (*starts forward, holding her breast, and squeaking*):
Oh! You! You—you'll make me die of heart
failure, anyone can see. Where did you learn these
tricks? Behaving like a ghost.

OLD WOMAN (*in a whisper*): I was a hospital nurse before
the war.

MITSOU: You've got some deaths on your conscience
then. Deaths from a stroke. Give me that lance!

She picks up a wooden lance wreathed in roses, and
looks at her own flower-like image in the glass. On a
very young face, is there much difference between a
look of passive peace and a look of hopelessness? . . .
Fluff bursts in, waving a postcard and jumping with
both feet at once.

FLUFF (*squealing*): I've got it, I've got it! Names
addresses, Army unit, everything!

MITSOU: Have they gone, then?

FLUFF: Gone? We can't get rid of them. They say it's

much more amusing here than in the audience.
I'll do my piece and rush upstairs again.

MITSOU: Where are they?

FLUFF: In Christophette Colombe's hanging-cupboard.
What a do, ducky! We're passing them pints of
beer through the curtain—and sandwiches—and
laughing our heads off.

She runs off quacking with pleasure. Mitsou goes
towards the stage, with the chastened and resigned
expression of a good little girl.

Two days later. *Scene:* the same. Ten o'clock. Mitsou is putting on the costume she wears in the final scene—the Pageant of Victory in red. The costume consists of a wisp of flame-coloured muslin and a sort of belly-band of crimson velvet. There is also a wooden sword, painted silver.

MITSOU (*yawning*): I don't know what's wrong with me tonight. My stomach's all knotted up, and I've a pain in the scallops round my ribs. I must have eaten too many calories, as my gentleman friend says. (*The Old Woman, still with her decoration and wooden shoes, shakes a dissenting head.*) You? Do you know what calories are?

OLD WOMAN: Of course I do.

MITSOU: Well, I don't; when my gentleman friend explains calories to me I always think I'm going to understand, and then just at the same moment it always all collapses—(*dreamily*) like everything else, for that matter. He never has any luck with me. (*A silence. Mitsou looks at herself in the glass. Then suddenly*—) And anyway I'm sick of all this red! Red always! Jacqueminot Rose first, then the Red Heart of Victory—blast it! How far've they got, down there?

OLD WOMAN (*learned and witty*): *Chi lo sa?*

MITSOU: You can cut that out; it doesn't impress me. Open the door so's we can hear.

OLD WOMAN (*having opened the door*): It's the number "Tropical Fruits". I can hear Miss Bit-of-Fluff's voice.

MITSOU: Yes, you've got good ears. (*Silence. A knock.*) Who's there?

A VOICE: Parcel for Miss Mitsou. (*The Old Woman receives the parcel, hands it to Mitsou. Mitsou turns it over and over, and at last undoes it. Inside are two flasks and a jar for powder, all of fine cut glass. Also a letter.*)

MITSOU (*reading aloud slowly*):

Madame,—This is the lieutenant in blue, by himself, for my khaki friend's leave was up before mine. The evening before last I realized when I left the music-hall that you must have spent all your month's salary on buying the 16 H.P. Renouhard that was waiting for you. The face powder in your dressing-room was bursting out of its box, and the bottle of lavender water still had the Bon Marché label on it. As a way of thanking you for a hospitality which was forced on you, I wonder if you would be willing to put both the powder and the scent in this glassware? It's not very expensive but—if I may break the truth to you gently—there's a war on.

Your most obedient servant,
The Lieutenant in Blue.

MITSOU (*having read this with difficulty, looks at the three glass objects, then at the letter, then at the objects, and then starts re-reading the letter in an undertone*): Madame,—This is the lieutenant in blue, by himself—— (*In a louder voice, to the Old Woman*) What does he mean by calling me Madame?

OLD WOMAN: He's being tactful.

MITSOU: It may be tact, but it's not polite. Give me that powder-pot and I'll put my powder in it.

OLD WOMAN: It's not a powder-pot.

MITSOU: Not a powder-pot?

OLD WOMAN: No. It's a jam-pot.

MITSOU (*outraged*): A jam-pot! Why don't you call it a coffee-pot and have done?

OLD WOMAN (*obstinate*): Because it *is* a jam-pot. It's a glass jar to put jam in, a Restoration piece and very pretty too. But I suppose you can put powder in it.

MITSOU: So nice of you to give me permission. (*Bell rings in the corridor. Mitsou gets up in a rush*) I'm on. I'm on. Quick, give me my sword. If it isn't too much trouble while I'm on stage, will you put the powder in the jam-jar and the lavender water in the flasks? Put it in both of them, so's they're filled up to the same level.

She goes out. The Old Woman behaves in a most unnatural manner. That is to say, she does fill the flasks up, and doesn't steal any scent for her own handkerchief or to put in a little bottle for herself. Even though she is by herself, she neither snorts, nor belches, nor picks her nose, nor reads the letter lying on the table, nor even pinches the cotton wool. Obviously, she is one of the remarkable characters thrown up by the war. There is a knock.

OLD WOMAN (*swiftly hiding the letter and envelope in the pocket of her apron*): Come in.

THE RESPECTABLE MAN (*handsome, as ever; and fifty, as ever*): Miss Mitsou on the stage?

OLD WOMAN: Yes, sir. Victory in Red, sir.

THE RESPECTABLE MAN (*stopping in front of the glassware*): What are those?

OLD WOMAN: Two flasks and a powder-jar, sir. I call it a powder-jar, sir, but as a matter of fact——

THE RESPECTABLE MAN (*interrupting*): I mean where do they come from?

OLD WOMAN: Dauvel's, sir. You can see the label.

THE RESPECTABLE MAN (*impatiently*): Who sent them to her?

OLD WOMAN: I don't know, sir. Perhaps Miss Mitsou bought them herself. She's certainly not very well off for things on her dressing-table; look at what——

THE RESPECTABLE MAN: Not well off? The whole place is a disgrace! I've wanted a hundred times to . . . But she always told me that a music-hall dressing-

room was . . . And that, anyhow, for a show about
the war . . .

OLD WOMAN (*touched*): Oh, she has such a warm heart!

THE RESPECTABLE MAN (*carrying on*): . . . for a show
about the war that quite likely wouldn't last more
than a fortnight. . . . (*He walks up and down in a
state.*) I tell you, I've been very firm. . . . I have a
furnishing firm which was going to . . .

Once more his sentence peters out. The Respectable
Man starts sentences excellently, and easily, but he
hardly ever ends them. A silence. Re-enter Mitsou,
who comes out of Red Victory as if it had been a
Turkish bath. On the way she has undone her tiny
crimson girdle, taken off her crown of gilt laurels, and
is dragging her silver sword behind her like a broom-
stick.

MITSOU (*opening the door and panting*): Oo! There isn't
half a crowd out there tonight. (*Seeing her friend.*)
Oh, there you are.

THE RESPECTABLE MAN (*kissing her hand*): My little dear!
How are you?

MITSOU (*who has seen the letter has vanished*): Hot. As you
can see. Have you got a season ticket here? Or
are you running after Fluff? (*She sits down and takes
off her shoes with a sigh—not a sentimental sigh at all.*)
Oh, my feet, my feet! (*She is watching the Respectable
Man's face in the glass.*)

THE RESPECTABLE MAN: Mitsou.

MITSOU (*taking off her make-up*): Here I am.

THE RESPECTABLE MAN: I didn't know you had this glassware.

MITSOU: I didn't either.

THE RESPECTABLE MAN: Did you buy them yourself?

MITSOU: Do I have to do my own shopping too?

THE RESPECTABLE MAN: Then in that case . . . From whom or from what . . . what is the meaning . . .

MITSOU (*looking like a dissolving rose under the vaseline*): A gift from an admirer.

THE RESPECTABLE MAN: From a what?

MITSOU: Just from an admirer.

THE RESPECTABLE MAN: Oh. Indeed. Well, this admirer, Mitsou. May one know his name?

MITSOU: You may perhaps. I don't.

Suddenly she realizes that she has spoken the exact truth, and it doesn't sound like it at all. She exchanges a sparkling look with her reflexion in the glass; behind her eyes is a laughing imp, and a new one—the imp of craftiness.

THE RESPECTABLE MAN (*vexed*): Madam is pleased to jest.

MITSOU (*turning round, and in an unexpectedly sharp voice*): "Madam!" What do you mean, "Madam"? Why are you calling me that?

THE RESPECTABLE MAN (*startled*): Why, Mitsou! It's just a way of speaking. . . . One says 'Madam is pleased to jest' as one says 'Madam is too kind'.

MITSOU (*stiffly*)ː Oh, is it? It so happens that to-night I am not pleased to jest, and I am not too kind.

THE RESPECTABLE MAN: Oh, Mitsou!

MITSOU (*working herself up*): So it's true, then!

THE RESPECTABLE MAN: What's true?

MITSOU (*as before*): It's true that you pick on me. You demand to know who sent me that glass. I reply to you "I don't know", because I *don't* know. I don't make a habit of telling stories: I'm not that sort of girl. You know quite well, if I get flowers on the opening night, or anything at all, I always show you the cards and the messages. Don't I?

THE RESPECTABLE MAN: Yes, yes, Mitsou; you do.

MITSOU: Very well then! So when I tell you I don't know who sent me this—this (*an anxious look at the Old Woman*) this jam-jar, the reason is that I don't know. Is that clear?

THE RESPECTABLE MAN (*who hasn't heard anything like this in three years which passed without a cloud, and without any sunshine either*): Of course it is, Mitsou! My little dear, don't worry! It's the heat. . . . And three matinées a week too. Tomorrow I'll have them send to your dressing-room a flask of a special 1848 brandy. . . .

MITSOU (*nervous, dressing herself*): No, no! Not any more flasks, for goodness' sake. Let's go! (*Looking at her room with hatred.*) It's disgusting in here! The wallpaper is filthy and insanitary. The table makes me sick. Pff!

THE RESPECTABLE MAN: But you never would allow me . . . I'll have the furnishing firm send to-morrow to . . . (*A knock.*)

MITSOU (*very overwrought, and jumping*): Who is that? Who is that?

A VOICE: Madame Mitsou?

MITSOU: Yes. What of it?

A VOICE: A message from madam's chauffeur. He will wait for madam at the corner of the street with madam's car, because the police have refused to allow him to park where he usually waits for madam.

THE RESPECTABLE MAN: Thank you very much, my man. (*He opens the door slightly and hands out a tip. As he turns round again, he is astounded to see tears in Mitsou's eyes.*) My little dear! What is the matter?

MITSOU: Nothing at all . . . (*Stammering*) It's . . . it's . . . it's the heat . . . and then, three matinées all in one week (*suddenly bursting into tears*) . . . and then too what do they mean by it? All these beasts tonight, all calling me madam! (*She goes downstairs crying, the Respectable Man following her in great distress.*)

III

Mitsou's apartment. A ground floor flat with "every convenience"— every convenience that can be bought for 3,000 francs rent in the Trocadero district. Two fairly large rooms looking on the street, two smaller rooms looking on the courtyard. The courtyard, of course, is "a large, very light square adorned with green trees". The bathroom, cupboards, kitchen and usual offices form a sort of indeterminate zone between the courtyard and the street, rather ill-lit, partly by electricity and partly by blueish daylight filtering in between two service lifts. In this indeterminate zone you breathe the inevitable and dismal smell of wine cellars, gas, clean sinks and metal polish.

Mitsou's furniture is extraordinary, but her intentions were impeccable. Ever since she has had enough money she has collected round her, with a sort of humble greediness, all the things she longed for in her poverty-stricken childhood. Everything is there. There is an electric-light Gothic crown in copper hanging over the dining table, whose glass jewels flash colours on to the elegant monogrammed dinner service in white and gold. And damask table linen, my dear! And a double bed decorated with garlands, on to which two carved cherubs drop from the ceiling a cascade of embroidered tulle. And a chaise-longue in three pieces (it would be better in a thousand pieces) all in silk damask. There is even, next to it, a small lady's desk to which you feel you ought to say kindly: "This isn't the right place; you've come to the wrong floor", it is so unexpectedly delicate and full of years and grace, pink like a dried rose.

If the sheets on the bed aren't as fine as they might be, Mitsou has increased the value of their ordinariness by hemstitching and adding fine lace a foot long. You would not expect or wish any other colours than blue and white in the bathroom, or that the modern, "so practical", dressing-table would be anything but one of those masterpieces of metalwork which combine the beauties of a dentist's chair and an American office desk. As for the parlour—no, I shall not describe the parlour. I have distressed you enough already. But take just a glimpse among the true or fake Dresden figures, the Louis XV bric-à-brac and the ornamented snuff boxes—take just a glimpse of the fat arrogance of that new-art cushion, splodged like a clown's face, and striped like a railway signal, like a jockey's cap, like a make-up towel that's been used all the week. Back away from a combination sofa and bookcase, in embossed bronze, violet plush, painted whitewood and mother of pearl . . . come and find Mitsou in her boudoir (looking on the courtyard) next to her bedroom (the same). The sun shines uselessly into the parlour and dining-room; they are shrines reserved by Mitsou for "company", which means she never sets foot in them.

It is half-past eleven. Mitsou in the morning is doing her housework; she is armed with that pointless weapon which cleans nothing and never dirties its user, a feather duster. She pats the treasures in her boudoir with it. She is wearing pink pyjamas, with tight tulle ruffles at the ankles, wrists and neck, and has a "Chinese" hairdo.

MITSOU (*to the maid*): If I've told you once I've told you twenty times; it's the electric lamps that go farthest from the clock and the candlesticks nearest.

THE MAID (*who looks like all maids who don't get enough sleep*): Oh yes. So it is. I never remember

MITSOU (*looking at her*): You look as if you've got indigestion today.

THE MAID (*simply*): No, ma'am; it's just that my fiancé's seven-days leave ended this morning.

MITSOU: Oh. Is it still the same fiancé? The sergeant?

THE MAID: Yes, the same one. Only he's a second lieutenant now.

MITSOU (*alert*): Oh, is he? How is he dressed?

THE MAID (*surprised*): Dressed? Why, dressed like a second lieutenant in the Zouaves.

MITSOU (*not interested now*): Oh, of course, a Zouave.

Zouaves don't wear blue. (*The telephone rings*). Will you see who that is?

THE MAID (*returning*): It was monsieur, to tell madam he will not be coming to lunch. The shareholders' meeting is going on too long.

MITSOU (*who doesn't care*): Goody. (*Humming*) Goody-goody-goody-goody-good. . . . You can tell Julienne not to bother with the aubergines. I don't care about them.

Silence. More dusting. Mitsou doesn't know anything at all about real housework. She can arrange flowers in a pot, and after three attempts can get a curtain's folds to fall right. But she doesn't know how to polish brass or copper, or give a looking-glass the sheen of clear water that it should have, or make mahogany shine with dark oil. She will learn these things, when wrinkles, plumpness and avarice first come to her.

MITSOU (*with a sudden cry*): Louise! (*The maid comes back.*) The result of all that is, I'm going to be quite alone for lunch.

THE MAID: As so often.

MITSOU (*crossly*): Yes, maybe as so often. But today, the way I feel, it'll spoil my appetite.

THE MAID: There is madam's mother who might be willing to come.

MITSOU: On a Saturday? It'd take more than a lunch for mummy to leave her Saturday customers.

Saturdays she does the Tarot cards for the Duchess
of Montmoreau, and tells tea-leaves for an alder-
man. Not a hope.

THE MAID: Madam has her singing master.

MITSOU (*disgusted*): Yes, and listen to his plate going
click-clack all the time he eats. You suggest the
horridest things. (*Brightening*) I know! Telephone
Miss Fluff and ask her to come to lunch.

THE MAID: Miss Fluff has got a telephone?

MITSOU: Yes. Wagram 6666.

THE MAID: Wagram 6666? That's the milkman.

MITSOU: The milkman? You're being funny.

THE MAID: I am not a funny person. I just rang that
number at eleven o'clock. Julienne had forgotten
to get the cheese.

MITSOU (*staggered*): Well . . . ring it all the same. I'll
swear I'm right.

THE MAID (*coming back, displeased and superior*): Miss
Fluff will come to lunch.

MITSOU: There you are! I told you.

THE MAID: Miss Fluff has a room at the back of the
milkman's. He lets her use his telephone. I said
she wasn't the sort of person to . . .

MITSOU (*interrupting, on her dignity*): the sort of person
to be waited on by a maid whose hair was all over
the place and with pillow feathers in it. Go and
comb it. I don't want to see ends in my house
when I never have a hair out of place myself.

The maid goes out. Mitsou whisks the dust off the glass of a showcase; it is no particular advantage that you can now see the contents more clearly. Then she dresses. It takes only five minutes because she is "all ready underneath" as they say. She has suède shoes, pink voile knickers and you can see her through her chemise as you can see a prize fruit through its muslin. Over it all she pulls a child's old fashioned dress, or rather an old fashioned child's dress, a green taffeta which has no cut, no waist, no shoulders, no anything —not even any skirt below the calf.

Mitsou is doing her nails—rather badly; that is to say, wasting a lot of colour and varnish—when Fluff arrives, with as much noise and fuss as a terrier. If she stayed still a moment you would notice that her jersey suit came from the cheapest department store, and her dented military cap had more cardboard than felt in it, and her shoes were almost worn out; but she never gives you time to observe all those details. She has a wide grey rabbit-fur collar which makes her summer suit "so chic" and comes right up to Fluff's eyes, which you can see are blue—or at least the eyelids are.

FLUFF (*falling back a step after the necessary kisses, squeaks and "darlings"*): What was it made you think of asking me to lunch?

MITSOU (*embarrassed*): Oh, I don't know. The fine weather, the . . . the aubergines. Do you like aubergines?

FLUFF: I can eat them.

MITSOU: I said to myself that you were sure to be the sort of person who liked aubergines. Now take off your fur; there's only the two of us; and your hat.

FLUFF: Your place *is* pretty. I've only been here before for a few moments in the evening; you can't see properly in artificial light. It's luck you don't have any sun in here; sun fades all the curtains, and the colours in pictures too aren't always fast.

MITSOU (*modestly*): Oh, there's nothing remarkable here. But it's all personal. I wouldn't let anyone advise me about choosing my things.

FLUFF: Nobody but you can know your own taste. You must never let any one else influence you when it comes to furnishing. Look at me; I've only got a tiny place, but if I'd listened to what people said to me I'd have thrown my collection away twenty times over.

MITSOU: Your collection of what?

FLUFF: My collection of souvenirs of travel.

MITSOU (*surprised*): Have you travelled a lot, then?

FLUFF: No, never. They're the travel souvenirs of people whom I've known. Before the war, I knew people from all over the place.

MITSOU: That must have been interesting.

FLUFF (*contemptuously*): Pooh! Don't talk to me of foreigners. Since the war started, I see life only in khaki—or in blue.

MITSOU (*quickly*): Well, now, that reminds me; I was just going to——

THE MAID: Lunch is served, madam.

MITSOU: After lunch I've got something to ask you.

She takes Fluff with her. Arm in arm they go, and sit down under the Gothic crown. Lunch: sardines, radishes; tasteless lemon sole; grey coloured beef and sodden potatoes; stuffed aubergines. Mitsou doesn't yet know either how to eat herself or how to arrange a dinner. The young ladies drink an excellent Chablis, it is true (a present from the Respectable Man), but they have no idea that it's good.

FLUFF (*looking at a plate*): They can say what they like, there's nothing like white porcelain for being distinguished, you know. Specially with an initial on. Your name—is that an Arab name you took?

MITSOU: No, it's my friend made it up. It's made out of initials. Pierre is managing-director of two companies; one is called *Minoteries Italo-Tarbaises,* and the other *Scieries Orléanaises Unifiées.* That makes M.I.T.S.O.U.; Mitsou.

FLUFF (*guffawing*): No!

MITSOU (*laughing too*): Yes!

FLUFF (*twisting herself*): Oh, oh, oh! And to think that I—what was it?—Oh, damn, I don't know, a friend I was introduced to the day before yesterday—anyway, I told him your name was Persian.

MITSOU: Persian?

FLUFF: Yes, you know, like the Russian ballet. Fancy that. (*They laugh.*) Oh, it does you good to laugh!

MITSOU: Yes, it cheers you up.

FLUFF: Why, do you want cheering up?

MITSOU (*reticently*): Not exactly. Just recently I've been feeling a bit off.

FLUFF: It's the time of the year. Me too, the theatre doctor listened to my chest the other day and told me I needed the country—fresh air, better food and a holiday. So I took his prescription out of his hands and signed it: "Wilson, Poincaré, Albert, George, Victor Emmanuel, exectera." Oh, Lord! country air and better food! Here's to the end of the war, and a motor car for me!

MITSOU: The country! I've never been in the country myself, except twice, when Pierre took me in the car. I'm a Parisian and the country makes me ill. The time when Pierre took me to the Loving Couple—don't get excited; it's the name of an hotel—I don't know what came over me. The sun setting, up there; and then the clouds; and the sky that seemed to go on for ever. It turned me up. I felt a sort of dizziness and stuffiness, a kind of choking, and I cried and cried. "Take me away", I kept saying to Pierre, "take me away; I think I'm going to die." It all went off in Paris.

I think the country doesn't agree with me, you know.

FLUFF (*whom the Chablis has made slightly tipsy*): Fresh air has a special effect on me. As soon as I get out in the country I want to go to bed.

MITSOU: Really! Does it make you as ill as that? (*Fluff's indecent laugh enlightens her.*) Oh, Fluff! Don't you ever think of anything but that?

FLUFF: Don't you think of it sometimes?

MITSOU (*tipsy too, but sad*): Well, yes, sometimes, before-hand . . . but never during.

FLUFF (*flinging her hands in the air*): My God! I suppose it'll always be true: making love is a poor man's pleasure.

MITSOU: Oh, I don't know. . . . I'm not rich even now, but I've been poor, and even then . . . (*She shakes her head, utterly disillusioned.*)

FLUFF (*interested*): Do you really mean that? I shouldn't have thought it was possible. Poor darling Mitsou, you're going to . . . (*because of the maid, who brings in the coffee*) you're going to dress shops that dress you much older than you ought to look. Go somewhere else.

MITSOU: I'm not the sort of customer who changes her tradesmen just for a fancy. Besides you know, the thought of moving, and changing—all the bother. I just stay sitting where I am.

FLUFF (*dirtily*): Sitting down—that isn't a practical

position. (*They laugh. She smells the coffee and the cassis.*) Good old coffee! I can do without anything, but not coffee. Got any sugar, Mitsou?

MITSOU: Of course.

FLUFF: Enough for me to have two cups?

MITSOU: Of course. A cup of coffee always means two cups.

FLUFF: Not in restaurants, it doesn't.

MITSOU: I've got some cigarettes; would you like one?

FLUFF (*boasting*): And so have I, thanking you. (*She lights one.*) Mine's Army tobacco too. It's those two pretty boys, the other night, who made me a present of them.

MITSOU (*taking the cigarette from Fluff's lips*): Show us, please? Which one gave you them? The khaki or the blue?

FLUFF: I really don't remember now.

MITSOU: You've seen them again? Did you . . . (*She stops.*)

FLUFF (*slack and sozzled, sipping a large glass of cassis*): Did I what? (*Mitsou says nothing.*) Oh, I see. No; have a bit of sense; there wasn't any time. They'd gone. It doesn't matter, though. I'll meet others, quite as good-looking.

MITSOU: Then you didn't . . .

FLUFF: No, I tell you, I didn't. I'd tell you if I did, wouldn't I?

(*A pause. Cigarettes, coffee, cassis.*)

MITSOU: You are nice, Fluff. We never seem to see each other.

FLUFF: When you work together, you don't have time to see each other.

MITSOU: How true that is! Think, about my friend: I've seen him every day for three years, and I haven't got anywhere, all the same.

FLUFF (*sententiously*): Yes, but it's bound to be so, in a case like that. A steady gentleman friend is like a guest. What can you talk about? His home, his business—they don't last long. "Good morning, dear, and how are the children? Has the youngest one quite got over his German measles? I don't like your partner's look. And the shareholders' meeting, was that amusing?" But a gigolo, a casual, a boy who takes your fancy, you know more about him in three-quarters of an hour than you do in three years about the other.

MITSOU: You don't say.

FLUFF (*firmly*): I'm telling you. In three-quarters of an hour—even less sometimes—you know how he makes love, you know if he's very cheerful afterwards, if he's short of money, if he's drawn his pay, if he likes your hat, if he knows your friends, if he bets, if he wants to see you again . . . in short, all the essentials. Even if you never see him again, he's a person, a memory, a man who really exists, you know.

MITSOU (*thoughtfully*): Yes, a memory. . . . And have you got a lot of them, these—these memories?

FLUFF (*pouring out some more cassis*): I should say so. And more to come.

MITSOU (*prudishly*): Oh, Fluff!

FLUFF (*quite tight now*): Oh, Fluff! Oh Fluff what? What's Fluff done? Certainly, more to come. Is it my fault if we're living in times like this?

MITSOU: Times like what?

FLUFF (*more and more exalted*): Times like I don't suppose anybody's ever seen since the world *was* the world! Have you ever seen a time before when the streets were packed with young fellows, all kinds of them, beautiful boys dressed to kill, looking at the girls and the grub and their mouths watering? Did you ever? Of course not. And are we supposed not to touch? To keep off the grass? And people denounce us and say "Women's shamelessness has no limits! the creatures hang round the necks of our sons and our husbands and our brothers and our cousins!" I answer them back. I say to those people, I say "Madam!"

MITSOU (*moved, drinking more cassis*): Who to?

FLUFF (*not hearing*): "Madam! I am not the sort of person to sew shirts for soldiers! I am no good at bandages. Nor for parcels for the prisoners, as I haven't got a bean. I am the sort of girl for you-know-what, and I wouldn't turn round to watch the lightning strike if a nice boy was in front of me. A nice boy, too, who might die tomorrow!"

MITSOU (*distressed*): Oh no, not tomorrow!

FLUFF (*going on*): "And, madam, unless you tie my arms and my legs, I am carrying on. And I shall open them, my arms, any moment I please, if I have a chance to make a boy happy even if it's only for ten minutes, if he's in khaki or if he's in blue!"

MITSOU (*with a squeal*): No, not the one in blue!

FLUFF (*brought down to earth*): What? What are you talking about? Who's in blue?

MITSOU (*distracted*): The one in blue! The one with the jam-pot! and the letter!

FLUFF (*leaves her chair and her cassis and runs to Mitsou*): Tell F-fluff, dearie; tell Fluff what it is.

MITSOU (*in a rush*): I want the address of the blue lieutenant that you put in my wardrobe and he sent me some glass and wrote to me and he didn't put his address on it (*She drops her head on to her folded arms.*)

FLUFF: Well, now, fancy that!

MITSOU (*raising her head and leaning against Fluff*): Now you understand. I know you've got his address. I didn't dare to ask you for it right away, Fluff; but do give it me, dear Fluff, please; please give me his address, please. (*She begins to cry.*)

FLUFF (*as if Mitsou had just earned a good conduct medal*):

Now that is nice! That is good, very good indeed!
Oh, excellent. You shall have it, of course you
shall. This is splendid.

She rocks her to and fro like a mother. Kisses,
whispers, planning. . . .

IV

Mitsou to the Blue Lieutenant

Dear Sir,—I do not know how to thank you for the
pretty things you sent me. I know enough about beautiful things to see that they were chosen by someone
with excellent taste. If you do me the honour of
coming to see me again, you will find many changes
in my dressing-room and you will see that your
pretty crystalware occupies the place of honour
there.

Very sincerely yours,

Mitsou

P.S. If I dared, I would like to ask you the date of your
next leave.

Blue Lieutenant to Mitsou

Madame,—You made a fool's bargain with me. To
send to you the most modest, ordinary triviality, and
to get in answer a letter in which humour, spontaneity
and Parisian grace all flower together—too much, it is
too much. How my comrades would envy me if I
showed them this letter, which they would certainly
say was the beginning of an adventure! You see, they
do not know that I am far from adventurous, and
that you embody in the revue at the Empyrée-

Montmartre, the gravity of youth, the determination to behave well—in short, Madame, Propriety with a big P, a motor car and a reliable gentleman friend. Is there anything I have forgotten? I beg your pardon if so, with all the modesty of a man whose surname and Christian name you know, but who still obstinately prefers to remain your anonymous and respectful

Blue Lieutenant

Mitsou to Blue Lieutenant

. Dear Sir,—I was very pleased to get your letter. It took only four days to come, which isn't much as things go nowadays—and they don't go very fast. Now and again some days are longer than others, you can't say why. Sometimes too there are compliments that don't please you and even make you sad; I thought that when I read your letter. I got more pleasure out of looking at your lovely handwriting than reading your letter, where there were bits that suggested you thought I was somebody else. If you wrote them in the hope that I wouldn't be able to understand them, it wasn't an awfully smart amusement for a young man like you. And if you thought I would understand them and be offended, then I can tell you I'm not upset, and a woman hasn't the time to be touchy when she has something else to think of. At least I've found out

from your letter what French officers mean by propriety—a tulle chemise and strawberry stockings.

I say "no hard feelings" to you and *au revoir,* and
don't forget next time that I asked for the date of your
next leave.

Mitsou

Blue Lieutenant to Mitsou

Madame,—Few female letter writers could boast as
you can of so many essentials in fifteen lines of handwriting: irony, the knowledge of what is correct,
mystery. The Mystery of the Music-hall Star! What a
title for a film serial in twenty-three reels! So those
eyes, wide open at life passing by, were lying, were
they? Thought was going on behind them! As for
irony, I have no right to be surprised at it, or I shall
look an ill-mannered lout again. It is the natural result
of living in the feverish atmosphere of the music-hall,
and in the company of those jolly dogs, the Writers of
Revues! I knew one once; he was a sparkling bureau-
crat long past the age of even a reservist. He filled a
counterfoil book every day with notes under the
headings *Newsvalue, Indecency,* and *Lavatory Jokes.*
Alphabetically.

As for my next leave, the Germans will fix the date
of it. If they behave themselves, two months; if they
attack, maybe never. Isn't it disgusting that my visit

to your dressing-room should depend on people like these?

I remain, Madame, most respectfully your
                                    Blue Lieutenant

Mitsou to Blue Lieutenant

You have chosen it, Sir, you are my Blue Lieutenant. See how funny words are. If I say "my lieutenant", it's nothing, but if I write "my blue lieutenant", it becomes nice. Fluff called one of her boy friends "my purple moorhen", but I'm not comparing that. I would rather you called me Miss Mitsou than Madame; I have no reason except that I don't like it.

I didn't find any "essentials" myself in your letter. Perhaps you didn't put any in. Except maybe the place where you were scoring off the poor old boys who write revues. That passage rather flattered me; it made me think I was talking to your respected father. Middleaged men like to make jokes about theatrical life as if they knew what goes on backstage, with little tee-hees and sniggers.

But when I read it again I saw it must be you. I saw you again just as you were in the wardrobe, and just as young. A young man must be very young not to know that when a woman tells him she is thinking of *something else* she really means *someone else*. Goodbye, my

Blue Lieutenant. Fluff sends you her best wishes, and
I am praying nothing will happen to you.

Mitsou

Blue Lieutenant to Mitsou

Miss Mitsou, I think today I shall possibly write
nothing but nonsense to you. One should never write
to a girl after two sleepless nights, for one of which I
was on guard duty. Miss Mitsou, your simplicity, your
apparent simplicity intrigues me more than I like. So
you spend your time thinking, do you? It's typical of
our age group—class 13 isn't it? Me too; I think. I
think about the family I belong to, about my job as a
soldier, about the swift and rather brutish pleasures of
my leaves and about—my pen-pal, you are going to
bet. Then don't bet. I haven't got, and I don't want,
a pen-pal. My friends, my comrades and my men, have
let themselves go in such an epistolary orgy, such a
wastefulness and gobbling of pen-pals that I stand
aside, glutted by the hoggishness before I start. But
what about you, Thinking Mitsou? Is it the pleasant
face of my khaki friend that haunts you? How silly of
me! It is, it must be, a civilian. We others, we just pass
by, we are running already when we throw behind us
a "Cheeri-oh . . . see you some time . . . maybe"; we
promise, the civilians keep our promises. They are
there—they are all there—what an advantage over us!

Perhaps your next letter will promote me to the rank of Confidant. It is correct; it is "the war", that a young Confidant, twenty-four years old and in the trenches, should listen to the romance of a matinée idol old enough to be his father. Miss Mitsou, I am all attention. I am prejudiced in your favour by a phrase that fell from your thoughtless pen, just at the moment I needed to read it: "I am praying that nothing happens to you."

Your respectful and tired
Blue Lieutenant

Mitsou to Blue Lieutenant

My Blue Lieutenant,—I couldn't help laughing when I read your letter, first of all because I was so pleased from the moment I saw the envelope, and next because you said "a phrase that fell from your thoughtless pen". Goodness! My thoughtless pen! It's obvious to see that writing comes easy to you. How could my pen be thoughtless, when I have to think of everything when I'm writing, spelling, handwriting, and what it is I want to say to you. Oh no, I'm never thoughtless in writing to you. And it's not just now when you're beginning to think not too badly of me that I'd let myself go.

So my letters don't bore you all that? What do you think I'd say of yours, then? What you don't guess is

that I've never corresponded with anybody before.
I'm a Parisian and I don't move out of Paris. All the
people I know are Parisian too, and for Parisians it's
much easier to spend twopence on the telephone than
write a letter. I would like to impress on you that it's
really something in my life for me to start writing
letters, and letters to you too. It's difficult for me to
understand the difference between the letters I do
write and the sort of letters you ought to be getting.
But anyway I do write to you truthfully. And however
silly Mitsou is, she will have sense enough to know
when the time has come that she ought to stop writing
to you. Thank goodness, that's the sort of thing one
learns without needing lessons in grammar.

I admit I did try to tease you a little in my earlier
letters. All right, and why not? The little I saw of you,
you did seem so young to me, so solemn, almost a
man-Mitsou. Like Mitsou you are afraid people will
let you down, like her you take your job seriously and
maybe like her you say: "Let's never forget we are
twenty-four years old, and that playing the fool is for
the elderly!" Because of the picture I've made of you,
I have the idea that I ought to of forgiven you everything but not to of forgotten anything. Anyhow I like
to think we are rivals in a way, rivals like friends or
twins I mean. It gives me a bit of courage, that is
courage enough to ask some questions. Questions like
for example:

1. Is night duty really dangerous?

2. Could you do with some useless things? Because one's family always remembers to send you the really useful things, but not the others. I'd like very much to send you things that aren't at all necessary but would amuse you.

The weather is lovely in Paris now. I hope it's lovely with you, and especially I hope it's lovely two months from now, or I ought to say exactly a month and a half. I take advantage of the fine weather and get up at ten o'clock; you'll say that isn't so early; but there's no reason for me to get up earlier; there's no post before ten. I asked. There's another at twelve, and that's very convenient, because the person you met in my dressing-room comes to lunch at one and I like to have my letters before then. Afterwards I can go out shopping, or anything; I can do what I like; there's no post, I mean no post that brings anything, until seven o'clock or half-past.

At half-past six I eat a big high-tea, and as the post is very unreliable just now it sometimes happens I find a letter after I come back home after the performance. This is what happened with your last letter, and I was as excited by it as if I'd found a real living person in my room.

Now here I am writing you a very long and silly letter, but I liked so much writing it that I can't bear to tear it up. Goodnight, Blue Lieutenant, I am

thinking of you and hoping that this is not going to
be another guard night.

Mitsou

Blue Lieutenant to Mitsou

I got your letter, Mitsou. I am reading it again; I am
so astonished that a small young woman who goes
around so easily with nothing on could hide so much
of herself. I haven't forgotten, Mitsou, and I shan't
forget all the details of the beautiful form that you
let me watch, with such arrogant indifference, from
the back of your wardrobe. But it wasn't while I was
staring at you that I felt like calling out: "What sort
of a person are you, Mitsou?" That is what I'm asking
you now, though; just as if we'd never met. Mitsou
with no grace of style, Mitsou with a schoolgirl's handwriting, you've never once failed to convey to me in
your letters just exactly what you wanted to say, nothing
more nor less. You didn't answer me, Mitsou, when
I asked you with a falsely indifferent air about the
person who occupied your private thoughts. No, you
didn't answer; you just gave me a very exact timetable
of the postal deliveries in Paris.

Cunning Mitsou! You have just shown me how
romantic even a railway timetable can be. It's both the
most annoying and most charming moment in an
affaire, when two beings who hardly know each other

yet, already have an inescapable compulsion to be together at a given time. . . . Mitsou, I am just going to call you Mitsou and nothing else. One word more, Mitsou, and I shall call you *tu*. No, I won't. The first *tu* should be a sudden cry which you can't resist; and there are no cries in a letter.

Why no, dear Mitsou, a night's guard isn't dangerous. But all the same, it is a trial; you carry two burdens that the long night makes very heavy. They are: responsibility and loneliness. Responsibility is the lighter of them; you know what it is, you know its limits, and you can face up to it. But loneliness fills you with dreams, with fears, with desires that you stamp on and reactions you suppress. In fact, it is unwise even to talk of them.

Do you really want to present me with what Richard Wagner—and he used French, by God—called the *enivrant superflu*? (He hadn't thought of your vivid phrase "Could you do with some useless things?") Yes, then; I could do with these useless things:

(1) A photograph of Mitsou.

(2) A piece of strawberry coloured velvet, the size of both my hands together, to be used to bind a book I am fond of. The exact shade to be that of Rose Jacqueminot.

That will be all for now. But my demands are by no means finished; tremble! Dear Mitsou, I kiss your long pretty paws respectfully and remain your

Blue Lieutenant

Mitsou to Blue Lieutenant

Dear Blue Lieutenant,—Lots of women when they got your letter would have imagined they were getting a love letter. But not me, thank goodness. In spite of the difficult words that I sometimes find in your letters there's no danger of my not understanding what they really mean. I'm flattered enough by them anyway not to start looking for impossibilities.

The picture of Mitsou and the velvet are going to you in a separate little parcel. The velvet is a good match; and the photograph is of "Rose Jacqueminot" too. But all that red is very depressing in a photograph. I don't want any parts in red any more; they make me dismal. Fluff wanted me to send you a little life-saving purse, like she sends to her boy friends. They're little purses in which she puts nothing but kisses. But I'm only sending you, as I did before, my true prayer that nothing will happen to you. The phrase has come back to me from the days when I had to write New Year messages on beautiful decorated notepaper when I was a little girl. I'm awfully sorry I can't invent a better one for you. My prayer is better than a fine phrase, because a phrase isn't anything real, and *it* is. It is as real as the swallow or the dove was on the fancy paper. I can see it, it flies around, it moves and has a face, it's all round you, on your head and on your breast—I can see it just as well as if I was there too, on your breast I mean. Fluff's purse would certainly be very pretty and lovely embroidered, but it wouldn't cover enough area. With my prayer, I'm less worried; it covers you all over.

You aren't half funny, dear blue lieutenant, asking me "Who are you, Mitsou?" I never expected to see you in the part of the compère in the revue who asks "But who is this beautiful girl?" If I was still in the Christmas revue at the Concert Mayol I would be wearing two wings, a helmet and a lance, and I'd answer "I am the Spirit of Heroic Love!"

But I am not the spirit of heroic love. I promise you I'm nothing out of the ordinary. You saw all of me on the wardrobe night; a small music-hall artist, young, not awfully ugly, popular with the public and without much talent. Now does this modesty surprise you? Oh come on, all we music-hall girls know very well where we are, in spite of the airs we seem to put on. Look at Fluff; she has found a line of her own by never for a moment staying still, "here I am and there I've gone". Now I'm a child type, I've got a nice innocent face, and eyes I open so wide it almost hurts my forehead, because that goes with my long legs and my small mouth and my almost-no-nose, and so the revue writers said "She'll be a smasher in the risky numbers; keep them for her!" See how simple it is. You haven't got a revue writer's mind, so don't try to see further than you have seen. I undressed in front of you, did I? Well, that shows I saw no harm in it, or I'd 've put

up the screen. I hardly spoke to you at all? It's only
that I was behind the door when tongues were given
out, as they say. To show you, I couldn't think of a
word to say when you-know-who came into the
dressing-room. That's really all. All about Mitsou
who was a good little garment worker and got frightened of the two things she knew best, poverty and the
workshop. So she took a fancy for the thing she knew
least about, the stage. Everybody always thinks it
easier to succeed in what they haven't learnt to do than
the things they have learnt; it's natural.

As for the rest, my private life, you know it. You
know who it depends on, or does until the day comes
when I decide it shan't depend on him any more. My
friends? It wouldn't take long to make the rounds of
them. I'm too young to have men friends, at my age it
gets spoilt at once. Women friends aren't easy either.
You run into bad lots who have got no decency. They
drink and they smoke opium. I know some who became typists or telephonists in a Ministry, but now
they treat us others like dirt. Of course I meet others
too who are just like me and they're the worst. After
being with them an hour I say to myself: "Now, is that
what I'm like? Am I like them already at my age, so
colourless, so absolutely dull off stage? Better stay at
home and stare in my mirror, it'll make me feel less
bad." Well, there! It's quite easy to learn to live alone,
at anyrate until something important happens. There's

only three important things that could happen in the lives of people like us—death, a great success on the stage, or love. Dear blue lieutenant, which is going to fall first on my head, or on my heart? I wish I knew.

No, don't kiss my hands, not even in a letter. They're not nice enough; the liquid white ruins the skin and besides I've put too much varnish on the nails. I'm looking after them, and I'll have them alright when you come. But kiss the crook of my arm; it has a lot of tiny rivers in blue and green and when you kiss it you need only be thinking of the army maps.

Your
Mitsou

P.S. But I too want a photograph!

Blue Lieutenant to Mitsou

Dear Mitsou,—I want to see you. I want to see you. What else is there to say to you? I want to see you. I feel gentle, weak, vague, turning towards something sweet, profound and indistinct that is calling me. I feel happy and yet deprived of everything, all at the same time. Anxiety and laziness too—both of them rather agreeable. An adolescent condition, I suppose. . . . Your photograph reminds me of two things—you; and a phrase of Francis Jammes about a young girl who "looked like a dark little rose, and was singing". . . . Mitsou, will you kiss me? I am asking you that because

I would like it. Our long previous acquaintance, of eight whole weeks of truthfulness, compels me not to hide anything from you. Kiss me, Mitsou. When I think that I fastened a belt behind your back, taking care not to nip in the hooks your skin so little covered by the tulle. . . . I remember that the petunia-coloured rouge on your cheeks, and the harsh lights, made your arms and the line down your back seem green, green like the white lilac that hothouses force to bloom in winter. . . . I remember that you quite coldly and chastely held up your slender arms to make it easy for me. . . . Mitsou, I don't like the smell of verbena. I only like one scent, the petals of a tea-rose dropped into a sandalwood box which has had very good tobacco in it; Mitsou's scent.

"A lot of changes in your dressing room?" Why? Wait a bit. Let me see it once again as I saw it *at that time,* from the back of the wardrobe. Don't change anything; only turn one piece of furniture out. A piece of furniture that came in while I was there, about fifty-five or fifty-six years old. A very bad period. Then everything will be all right. Dear, dear Mitsou, how I like everything about you, and especially how anxiously your letters describe for me your clean and sad life, as empty as a new attic! Do you know mine is almost as empty? Mitsou, we boys of twenty-four, the war grabbed us just as we came out of college. It made us into men, and I am afraid that we shall never recover from having missed the time of growing up. We lost forever that precious period, in which we might have learnt poise and balance in voice and manner, and the habit of being free, and how to treat our families and how to approach women without being afraid or acting like cannibals—women, I mean, who would not be thinking only of our desires or our money. Mitsou, forgive me for boring you with all this. The reason is that just now my regrets have a special reason: am I going to throw at your feet an overgrown schoolboy or a much-too-young grown man, who will be like a fruit out of season, ripe on one side and green on the other?

Mitsou, listen. In ten days, Mitsou, I—well, in ten days I am going to be in Paris for forty-eight hours, on a special service. The brutality of that statement shocks me. I am blushing over it, as one blushes over the movement of one's hand over a breast or a bottom in a crowd, which one's ashamed of afterwards.

Here's the photograph of me you wanted. It is yellowish and not mounted, and I look very ugly frowning into the sun. The small rise that you see in the distance through the opening in the earth wall is the German lines—only four hundred yards away, damn them. How nice that crimson velvet smells; I had it with me in bed.

Your
Blue Lieutenant

Mitsou to Blue Lieutenant

Dear Blue Lieutenant,—It's over now, the screwing
up my courage to write to you; I'm going to see you.
I've seen you already, in fact, in that photo you say is
horrid, and all the same I feel sure, I feel so sure my
head swims, that you chose it because you know how
wonderful you look against the sky-line, and it shows
your figure and the way you hold your head and stick
your chin out. No, don't, don't say it's horrid; it's
everything that I like and makes my heart beat faster.
You know, I give up, now. Do you know, I've been
holding myself back, ever since I wrote you that first
stupid letter; I'd have liked to write to you quite
simply: "I must see you again, because I've changed
altogether and I think I'm in love with you". But how
wise I was to hold back! First of all, it probably wasn't
true then that I was in love with you. I hadn't really
got the disease properly; it was like the beginning of
flu. I don't know what state I was in; I complained to
Fluff I kept going hot and cold; I asked the dresser for
stomach pills and headache pills. You see I just didn't
realize. Even your present you gave me, I looked at it
as if it'd done something to me; I picked on it and
nagged at it: "That blue lieutenant, I suppose he
thinks I'm going to run after him because of a powder
pot!" I mean, all sorts of stupidities and misinterpreta-
tions. I can't write clearly like you. However, as Fluff
says "Keep your mouth shut and you won't make

mistakes"; I am relying a lot on my silence, for when you come here and are near me. Look at me, in such a hurry to turn myself inside-out-like for you, as if I was a basket of fruit to show that what's underneath is as good as the top. It's because I've been full for the last two months of new thoughts so nice and so worrying that I can't find words good enough to describe them.

Only a little while ago I was sure I wouldn't be able to write to you. And as it is I don't think this letter will be right about all those things that seem to me so important and so urgent. I've only just this moment thought that you've never seen me in ordinary clothes. It's awful. I don't know what to do. You never said if you liked small hats, and I almost never were anything else. My skirts aren't very short, anyhow. I hardly ever were very bright colours in the street; it's not right in wartime and anyway I like to get away from the rainbow colours on the stage. What I were is navy blue, dark green, and black and white. I don't make my face up when I go out. My hats fit tight and I show my ears, because they're not large.

What else should I say? You've seen almost all the rest, and I wish you hadn't now. I really haven't anything seriously wrong with my body, except my toes a little bit, because of wearing fashionable shoes. And there's a scar, from an accident with a hatpin, on the back of my neck just where the hair begins. I shall never bow my head before you, though, unless I'm ashamed or sorry, so it only depends on us two and you mayn't ever see it.

I don't know what's going to happen to me. I don't know if anything is going to happen to us. . . . Oh yes, I do hope something will. We are very young and liable to everything. But before having really known you and even if you forget me quickly I want to say thank you from my heart. Perhaps quite soon I shall see in my mirror Mitsou laughing for joy. Perhaps it will be a Mitsou in tears. But whichever it is it won't be the same Mitsou as before you came, that stupid sensible Mitsou, who never laughed and never cried, that poor creature who didn't even have her own private sorrows. So I am your debtor for life, dear, dear Blue Lieutenant, because you couldn't help giving something to a girl who had nothing.

Your

Mitsou

V

Mitsou's flat. She is waiting for him. He ought to arrive in Paris at noon, but he has a family. He has promised Mitsou to come to tea, and she is waiting for him. Yesterday she bought an English teatable, some port, three lace aprons for the maid, 125 francs' worth of perfume, and a hat; and stood around for two hours for the "final fittings" of two frocks. This morning she bought fruit and flowers.

It is five o'clock. The scent is in the hairdressers' bottles and shines, with the colours of brandy and green chartreuse; cherry brandy, port and cognac are on the table and look like the golden toilet water and the liquid carmine that Mitsou uses to touch up her gums and the inside of her lips. The flowers are feeling the heat. The sun is moving slowly; it lights up the bowl of cherries, throws a circle of gold on the table and finally touches Mitsou's shoulder, in the armchair where she has been sitting for some time.

MITSOU (*getting up suddenly*): It's five o'clock! (*The sound of her voice alarms her; she repeats more quietly*) It's five o'clock.

She opens a picture-paper and puts it down again because she sees her hands are trembling. She tries to walk up and down, but there is no up-and-down in this boudoir, and she takes refuge by the window, against the lace curtain, knowing she has found the place that she won't move from, not until she hears the wheels of a vehicle, the sound of a horn and the banging of a taxi door, the ringing of a doorbell.

She is wearing a black satin dress, with emerald green embroidery at the neck and with short sleeves that stop, as Fluff says, where your arms get skinny. Mitsou is not very pretty today. All the same, her pale face with no make-up, her long heavy lashes, her smooth hair (black satin too) and the unfashionable but distinguished length of her swan-neck give her the solemness and black-and-white charm of a heroine of romance—though no heroine of romance would have so short a nose.

She is thirsty and bites her dry lips. She leans her forehead against the half-open window, enjoys the faint draught and thinks that a thousand tumultuous thoughts are running through her brain. In fact she isn't thinking about anything; she is just waiting. She stares into the street and sometimes looks down at her shoes, which have wooden heels. Now and again a small worry runs through the anxious emptiness of her mind, stings, and vanishes: "I think a thread has gone in my stocking. . . . I ought to have taken an aspirin. . . . Suppose he isn't free for dinner? . . . Suppose I meet Pierre in the restaurant? . . . And if he wants to come home with me tonight what shall I say? . . . I ought to have taken the black hat and not the black

and green. . . . It's half-past five. . . . Perhaps he has
been prevented from coming."

Suddenly the taxi has come. Mitsou just has time to
hear a voice ordering the taximan to "take three
francs". Two doors open, and shut. Now here he is in
front of her—and he doesn't recognize her. He has
pictured her a hundred times—against a sky ripped by
gun fire, against a moonless night, in a chequered
dream—as a Mitsou in town clothes or in pyjamas, or
in a dressing-gown. But in fact he has only seen her
once, rather imperfectly clothed in tulle and red stockings. He is surprised and a little embarrassed; he had
expected to arrive and cry "Mitsou!" and throw his
arms round some ruffled tulle and almost-bare flesh.
However, he finds her pretty and rather touching, a
young woman in black, rather pale, holding out her
hand to him.

But Mitsou has recognized him, every inch of him.
There is no surprise or disappointment for her. She is
smiling, simply out of pleasure because her blue
lieutenant's hair isn't as black as she thought—much
more dark brown, really, with a touch of auburn at
the neck. And she says at once just what she ought to:

MITSOU: How handsome you are!

He smiles and kisses the small hand held out to him
He is blushing and hasn't the courage to kiss the pale
cheek, downy with a faint dust of powder. Anyway,
Mitsou did not expect to be kissed. She sits down,

motions him to a chair, and starts conversation.

MITSOU: Did you have a good journey?

BLUE LIEUTENANT: A very good one, thank you. Of
course it was very slow. (*A pause.*)

MITSOU: Would you care for a glass of port?

BLUE LIEUTENANT: If you will drink too—yes, please.

MITSOU (*filling two glasses*): Cigarettes are next to you.

BLUE LIEUTENANT: If you will smoke too, yes please.

She lights a cigarette and blows out the smoke with
a great puff. He drinks. She drinks. She puts down her
glass with a trembling hand and smashes the stem.

MITSOU (*crying out as if the ceiling had fallen down*): Oh!

BLUE LIEUTENANT (*getting up*): At last! I was waiting
for that! (*He seizes Mitsou in his arms and starts
kissing her blindly.*)

MITSOU (*as soon as he lets her go*): It's plain glass.

BLUE LIEUTENANT: Now what on earth——

MITSOU (*breathing rather fast*): It means luck. (*She
cuddles back into his arms.*) Kiss me again, please.
While you're kissing me, at least I'm not frightened of you.

BLUE LIEUTENANT: Of course. I'm only doing it to
reassure you.

He continues to reassure her. Her cold hands grow
warm and unclench, the thin little body he holds
softens and seems almost lifeless. Mitsou shuts her
eyes, but the lieutenant looks at her and sees long eyelids edged with black eyelashes, then a forehead from

which the hair has fallen back, and beyond it the mantelpiece with bric-à-brac on it.

BLUE LIEUTENANT (*under his breath*): If I have a minute alone, there's a statuette here I'll smash myself.

MITSOU (*out of breath*): Ah! (*very quietly, and very cautiously*): Robert. . . .

He is as pleased as if he had been given a present. She has never called him Robert before.

ROBERT (*quietly*): Yes, Mitsou; it's me.

Whispering makes them more comfortable. They aren't yet used to the tones of each other's voice.

MITSOU: Well, here you are.

ROBERT: . . . .

MITSOU: Will you have dinner with me?

ROBERT: . . . .

MITSOU: But not here.

ROBERT (*brought back to earth*): But why not here?

MITSOU (*embarrassed*): Well, you see . . . (*He frowns slightly, for no special reason, and she begins to lie at once*) you see the food isn't good enough for you here, we eat just what comes.

ROBERT (*shocked*): Mitsou! Aren't you a gourmet?

MITSOU: Oh, yes, I am, really. But you can't get cakes anywhere.

ROBERT: Cakes aren't the only thing. What are we going to eat tonight? Come and sit on my knees and give your order. Curried lobster? Chicken and mushrooms?

MITSOU (*pouting*): No. What I want is cold salmon with an awful lot of mayonnaise. And then perhaps some sweetbreads. It doesn't matter. What is a nuisance is that we must dine early, because of the revue.

ROBERT: Is it still the same revue?

MITSOU: No, it's a new one since Friday.

ROBERT: Have you got good parts?

MITSOU: I should say so! I do the "Harem Dance", and "Liberty Shining through the World", without tights, and "A Girl of the Sixteenth".

ROBERT: Sixteenth century?

MITSOU: No, the sixteenth ward, the one which is next to the American camp at Auteuil, and you can guess how she earns her living.

ROBERT (*pensively*): Life is getting very odd.

A silence. He forgets to kiss Mitsou and starts looking round him. The clinical dressing-table fascinates him; he would like to ask Mitsou sympathetically: "How did you get that thing planted on you?" for he doesn't like to think she is responsible.

MITSOU: It's striking, isn't it?

ROBERT: What is, Mitsou?

MITSOU: My dressing-table. It was a very young artist who designed it; he just made that one only, and then he died.

ROBERT: Too late.

MITSOU: No, you don't understand. He died rather young, about thirty, I think.

ROBERT: Yes; I really should have said: Not soon
enough.

MITSOU (*all innocence*): No, I'm trying to explain to
you . . .

ROBERT: Darling, don't explain anything.

MITSOU (*with a rush of joy*): Oh, I do love to have you
in my own place. It is *really* my own place! Have
you noticed my glass cabinet? And the armchair
in silk? Bounce on the springs, do! And look
at the etchings! They're really old. Guaranteed.
Have you seen them?

ROBERT (*to himself, in a very gentle tone*): Yes. I've seen
them. There's no question. Every one will have
to be burnt.

MITSOU: Burnt?

She looks at him, and he stops. She has a way of
disarming sarcasm; when she doesn't understand she
falls silent and opens her big patient eyes, until the tips
of her eyelashes touch her eyebrows.

ROBERT (*touched*): Dear Mitsou!

He holds her close to him and for the minute thinks
that she really is dear to him, for he had very nearly
wounded her.

MITSOU (*relaxed*): Well . . . what are we going to do?

He was not expecting that question. However, he
lets his hands slip down from Mitsou's shoulders along
her arms, then down her thighs, pressing her obedient
young body so firmly that they don't seem to be

just caressing her, but moulding her, creating her.

MITSOU: No, no, no. I mean—that is, I only meant—
it's getting late.

ROBERT: Then I shall dine with you, Mitsou, if you
will do me that honour.

MITSOU (*seriously, and meaning it*): The honour is for me.

He drops his eyes and blushes a little under his tan,
as he does always when Mitsou so easily outdoes his
expectations.

ROBERT: I shall take you to your theatre, which is a
music-hall. . . .

MITSOU (*anxiously*): Yes?

ROBERT: And afterwards. . . . (*She says nothing.*) And
afterwards I shall deliver you at your front door.
(*Mitsou's eyes become suddenly bright with tears, and he
continues hastily, with a slightly sadistic compassion.*)
At your front door, and then I shall say to you
very confidentially: 'Mitsou, my mother's old
butler sleeps very very soundly, and I stand a
fair chance of spending the night on the doorstep,
unless——"

He stops. Neither of them feel like smiling, and
Mitsou does not lower her eyes. Her expression is so
little that of a woman, especially that of a woman in
love, it has so much decision, so much fatalism, so
little hope in it, that pity and once again a sort of
respect strike the young man's virgin heart. He comes
up to the level of her simpleness.

ROBERT: Mitsou, will you have me?

MITSOU: Oh, yes, with the greatest of pleasure.

Her awed young voice gives life to the tired cliché, and he notices that the phrase tactfully makes no reference to love.

VI

Restaurant lavoie. As it is only a quarter-past seven and several tables are still unoccupied, Mitsou and her lieutenant have secured a corner table in the best part of the restaurant (the left side) and even a certain amount of deference from the commissionaire and a waiter. It is still broad daylight and the rather airless room smells of melon and strawberries. Robert is looking delightedly at the heavy golden dust of the evening, which makes the sky behind the Madeleine a delicate green.

A PAGE (*twelve years old, and with the gravity of his years*): Bread coupons, please.

ROBERT: Never mind, Mitsou; I've got some.

MITSOU: So've I. I get extra as a nightworker.—Don't give him more than two; that's all we need.

ROBERT: But I'm hungry, Mitsou. Here you are, young man. (*The severe child goes away.*)

MITSOU: Are you all right there? Wouldn't you like my corner seat?

ROBERT: I'm very much all right here, Mitsou.

He looks around, with the slightly false aplomb of a man of the world of twenty-four. He puts on an expression of bad temper, to warn all the other guests not to stare at Mitsou, and also to indicate that he himself is quite accustomed to her, in fact hardly interested.

Having given this warning to two depressed Deputies, two ladies from the American Red Cross and a party of four bronzed and garrulous senior officers, he decides to turn his own eyes on Mitsou and enjoy the sight of her in a restaurant—Mitsou in a black hat with an emerald green coronet on it, Mitsou in a black satin cape falling from her shoulders and showing off her long, white, victim-like neck. Mitsou has suddenly become very pretty again.

ROBERT: Black does suit you, Mitsou.

At the same time he is asking himself a question: "Now, why is Mitsou, who is not made up, whose hair is not permed and is brushed away from her ears, who doesn't gesticulate, and hasn't raised her voice—why doesn't Mitsou look like what we call a lady?" This question is so difficult that he doesn't notice the head waiter who is standing next to him. The man's face is like an overfed Roman emperor's and you can read his thought; it is: "My time is precious. I will waste it without a thought, for the sake of my country. I will suffer in silence."

MITSOU (*flattered at Robert's attention*): Robert!

ROBERT: Oh! Yes, I'm sorry. Mitsou, wouldn't you like some lobster? I haven't had any for four months. *Homard a l'indienne?*

MITSOU: Oh, yes. With a lot of mayonnaise and both claws.

THE HEAD WAITER (*looking beyond the uttermost edge of*

this world of sorrows): *Homard a l'indienne* is not
served with mayonnaise. It is served with saffron
rice and curry.

MITSOU: Oh, I don't mind. Serve me the mayonnaise
separately.

ROBERT: Put down mayonnaise. Chicken with mushrooms—oh, good; they've got some. Mitsou, do
you like chicken?

MITSOU: Oh, yes, indeed; as long as there's salad with
it.

THE HEAD WAITER: The chicken with mushrooms is
not served with a salad; there is a cream sauce
with——

MITSOU: It doesn't matter. You can serve me a salad
separately.

THE HEAD WAITER (*reciting*): Strawberries, raspberries,
cherries in ice, bananas, fruit salad.

MITSOU (*gleefully*): Cherries in ice! Cherries in ice!

ROBERT: But they're not nice, Mitsou! They haven't
any taste at all.

MITSOU: That's just it; they're fun.

ROBERT: Cherries for Madame and for me (*greedily*)
wild strawberries with thick cream. Send me the
wine waiter. Mitsou, shall we have burgundy,
claret or champagne?

MITSOU: It's all the same to me; I don't care what countries wine comes from.

ROBERT: I think they've got a very attractive claret

here; it has a light bouquet of coffee and of violets in the glass.

MITSOU (*horrified*): How dreadful! Fancy a thing like that here!

ROBERT: I'm not suggesting burgundy, which wouldn't go with lobster, and is too full for the chicken——

MITSOU: Does burgundy sparkle?

ROBERT: People sometimes make it do so. But there. I can see we shall end up having champagne.

MITSOU: Oo, yes! A champagne that doesn't taste! (*The wine waiter is present and visible, but he has long lost any interest in the conversation.*)

ROBERT (*shocked*): That doesn't taste! Mitsou, where on earth were you brought up?

MITSOU (*annoyed, because of the wine waiter*): Not in a wineshop, anyway.

ROBERT (*to the wine waiter*): A bottle of ——, *brut.* Mineral water, Mitsou?

MITSOU: Yes, please! A fizzy one.

They are waiting for the lobster. The empty tables are filling up; the American element is in the majority. Fair officers, with red-apple cheeks, are admiring Mitsou inordinately—that is, they put down their glasses half full and look at her with their mouths dropping, and forget their drink. Robert frowns to hide his proprietary pleasure. Mitsou compares him to them all and thinks, "He's much handsomer". She is not wholly wrong; her lover is a delicate and brown type, with thin hands and little bones which move under a fine skin; his moustache, untrimmed, hides a short upper lip, that faintly pulls on his nose as he talks. His eyes are "awfully big for a man", Mitsou decides, and are sunk rather deeply and mysteriously in their sockets.

They are very young, solemn, and silent. She is contemplating him; he is watching her. They are not drunk; that will come later. And as a matter of fact here is the champagne, before the lobster. Mitsou draws the fizziness into her mouth, blinking; he drinks his glass right off.

MITSOU (*laughing*): It's better than the Army ration, isn't it?

He admits that important truth with just a nod. "There it is," he thinks, "I've found out what Mitsou needs. She's much prettier when she's sad than when she laughs. I ought to tell her sad sentimental stories, but I couldn't possibly. I wonder why. I used to write to her without troubling." He notices that he is not quite sure he wants to be Mitsou's lover tonight. "What a pig I am," he says to himself, just at the moment when the pig in him is weakening, the cheerful, greedy pig.

MITSOU (*to the waiter, who is serving her*): That's enough, thank you.

ROBERT (*protesting*): But you've only got one small claw.

MITSOU (*elegant*): I may have a second helping. But, you know, I'm not really fond of exotic food.

ROBERT (*laughing despite himself*): Mitsou, I would bet you've never seen the sea.

MITSOU: Yes, I have then. At Deauville. I was awfully bored.

ROBERT: I don't wonder you were.

MITSOU: It's true, isn't it? I'm so glad you said that. I didn't understand a thing about it.

ROBERT: About what?

MITSOU: About Deauville. Of course I was only two days there and I came just in the car. But I don't understand those sort of places where everyone is outside like that. I can understand you'd go to the casino, or to a tea-room, but not everyone always about as if no one had a home. . . .

ROBERT: Why, Mitsou, the fresh air! The sea! The wild waves of Deauville!

MITSOU (*shaking her head*): No, it doesn't say anything to me. I don't really care for the country. (*Looking at him*) But with you, perhaps! A bamboo hut with you, if you like.

ROBERT (*disarmed and encouraged*): Darling Mitsou! We *will* go to a bamboo hut. But not in a car—I haven't got a car.

MITSOU: I haven't either.

ROBERT: But I thought——

MITSOU: Oh, that's not mine, the one you saw. It

belongs to Pierre. He has to have one for his business.

ROBERT (*coldly*): I see.

MITSOU (*mildly, but insistently*): He has to do a lot of business—very fortunately.

ROBERT (*on edge*): Isn't there some other subject that you'd like my congratulations upon?

MITSOU (*candid*): Is congratulations the same thing as condolences?

ROBERT (*who is not going to joke*): No, Mitsou; it is not. And furthermore, don't you see that this person is not one that you should talk to me about? Elementary, my dear.

MITSOU (*who has, after all, drunk three glasses of champagne*): Oh, you are so touchy! Tomorrow morning, even if you haven't liked me during the night, I'll have given you anyway something I've never given anyone before.

ROBERT: . . . ?

MITSOU: No, I don't mean what you mean. I just mean —my love. It's not so difficult to understand; I've never been in love really before and now I am. That's all. So you see that person isn't really worth envying and you really haven't any reason to call him elementary.

He kisses her hand, and keeps in his hand her long, sensitive fingers—they are warm, and return his pressure honestly and eagerly, glad to trust themselves to

him. As he does this a weird half-hallucination comes
over him; he seems to be reading over and over again
the phrase Mitsou has just used, written up on an
empty space on the eastern wall of a trench and seen
by the light of a torch. "I've never been in love really
before and now I am." "I expect she'd have spelled
really with a double E. Well, then I love her double
Es." A nervous little summons by the hand he is
holding brings him back. "God forgive me, I really
believe I was forgetting Mitsou was there in front of me."

(*Aloud*): Wine waiter! Another bottle, please.

MITSOU: Another bottle! But you'll be tight! (*She bursts
out laughing for no reason at all. Flapping her arms like
wings—*) I'm hot, I'm not! Let's go!

ROBERT: Go! And leave the chicken, with its mushrooms, all alone? It'd be frightened. And, look,
here it comes!

MITSOU: And, look, here it comes! Why, that's a line
from one of my parts in the next revue.

ROBERT: Obviously, it'll be a uniquely original show.

The waiter serves. Mitsou eats but little, and Robert
eats less than he hoped. Their conversation becomes
feebler than ever; it is no more than some exclama-
tions, some hand squeezings and smiles of false understanding; their shouts of laughter hide the emptiness
of what they say. The guests at the next table are very
envious of this pair of lovers who are enjoying themselves so much. But the fact is that Robert is near to

despair, in spite of the champagne and the good food. He has held Mitsou's feet and knees between his boots; she submitted happily to the hard pressure of his cavalryman's knees. All the same, he does not desire her, not yet anyway. Indeed, he has no desire at all, except that he wants to go away, to go away—to see nothing in front of him but an empty street in the twilight, or a deserted avenue with young grass growing in it, or even one of those country roads where the verges have been trampled out of existence by lorries and armoured cars. Mitsou has so small a place in his wishes that he is getting hysterical. He starts hunting for excuses for lust and jealousy in the glances which the drunk but respectful Americans are throwing at Mitsou. He calls up pictures of Mitsou half naked and in her red stockings. He reproaches himself and works himself up; and it won't do. Suddenly he stops trying to be amusing or even nice. He notices, without any particular pleasure, that Mitsou when she is animated shines like a jewel, that the wine has not made her flushed, and that the nostrils in her over-small nose are still pale and transparent. He has no emotion while listening vaguely to her bringing out some family traditions as rules of life:

"The leaves of a mallow-plant are the things to cure drunkenness, mother always told me. . . . Let a man walk two steps alone and he'll do three silly things was what mother said. . . . Mother always taught me that you can't possibly **be** insulted by anything your inferiors say."

He is dreaming, hiding himself in a melancholy solitude. If he dared, he would throw down his napkin, put a banknote on the table, light a cigarette—and say "Goodbye!" Suddenly he hears with indescribable relief that Mitsou is asking him the time. He cheats, by five minutes.

MITSOU: Oh, dear! Is it that already? Darling, I've got to go to the Empyrée. Oh, it's beastly. And my head's spinning too.

ROBERT: Waiter! The bill, please. (*To the commissionaire*): My coat, please. (*He gets up too quickly.*)

MITSOU (*angel-faced*): Where are you going? Do you want to go round the corner? It's on the first floor.

ROBERT (*choking*): Round the——? Really, Mitsou!

MITSOU: Why not? Don't you ever want to go there?

ROBERT (*to recover himself*): The Queen of Spain has no legs, madam!

MITSOU: First I heard of it. Fancy the Spaniards not minding being ruled by a cripple. . . . Have I got my gloves? Yes, I've got my gloves. Have I got my bag? No, I haven't.

Robert is certainly rather drunk and is electrified by the attraction that Mitsou is securing; he hums the chorus of a popular song. As they walk through the restaurant Mitsou is struggling against dizziness and

assumes a look of elegant disdain, Robert an air of
devil-may-care which suits him about as well as a ball
dress would.

They come out into the street. The Madeleine is
pink in the slow-dying spring twilight. Children of
three to five years old are selling evening papers and
fading daffodils. Except that the daffodils cost a franc
instead of ten centimes it is just like peacetime. Mitsou
shivers. Robert stretches and breathes deeply; he has
come out into the open.

COMMISSIONAIRE (*to Robert*): Taxi, sir?

MITSOU: And quickly, too.

She hangs on to Robert's arm, while two commis-
sionaires start their usual evening hunt; this consists
of shooting down, at either end of the Rue Royale,
any flying taxi-birds. They run lightly, hardly earthbound at all; sometimes one leaps on to a taxi on the
wing, hangs on for a moment and drops off it to
attack a more hopeful prey. At last a vehicle is
captured, scrapes up to the kerb and stops.

ROBERT (*to the driver*): The Empyrée, Montmartre.

DRIVER (*sourly*): Is that all?

ROBERT (*with the cold assurance of a gentleman*): You will
    go where you are told. Get in, Mitsou.

MITSOU (*to the chauffeur, who is starting to speak*): I should
    jolly well think it was all. Do you think I could
    stand your face any longer?

Recognizing a colleague from her accent, the driver

starts up and says no more. Mitsou leans her head on Robert's shoulder; Robert's arm goes round her slender hips. This is the best minute of all. The fresher air, the speed, the bluish lights of the half-blacked-out gas-lamps, the alcohol running in their veins, for Robert Mitsou's scent, for Mitsou the novelty of a mouth that is kissing her mouth; all these are delicious. This is the first time that Mitsou has tasted, one by one, those smooth lips, that enterprising tongue, and those regular small teeth. There is a small canine tooth which is sharper than the others; the pleasure of its nip is so acute that Mitsou pulls herself away.

MITSOU (*head back and eyes shut*): Oh! I wonder where it was you bit me.

He presses her roughly back against the faded cushions and the quivering taxi-hood. He is glad to feel himself at last quite normally exasperated, hurried, and hardly with a thought for this woman that he wants. He does, though, remember her name and says in a low voice:

Mitsou!

MITSOU (*weakly*): Yes . . . But how can we? . . . We're nearly there. . . . Do let me go, we're nearly there. Let me go, let me go; you can see I haven't strength to stop you doing anything you want.

He doesn't hear her, and he doesn't stop; but the taxi pulls up in front of the funereal line of purple lamps which is all now that indicates a place of amusement.

MITSOU (*hesitating*): Aren't you coming?

ROBERT: Where?

MITSOU (*pointing to the stage door*): With me. To wait.

ROBERT (*cross and greedy*): No. You come.

MITSOU (*distressed*): But I can't! Think of my contract. Shall I give you the key?

ROBERT: What key?

MITSOU: The key of my flat, of course. You can go back there and get into bed and wait for me.

ROBERT (*shocked*): Certainly not.

MITSOU: (*still more upset*): But what will you do?

ROBERT: Walk about. Wait outside here. Go to the pictures.

MITSOU: Why don't you go into the audience and see my act?

ROBERT (*sullenly*): I don't know. I just don't like to watch you from the audience any more.

MITSOU (*annoyed*): Well, it's a pity. I've got such pretty costumes, and a very serious number called "The Ivy on the Battlefield" with a little girdle of ivy leaves and a matching crown.

ROBERT (*with a loud laugh*): Well, that's funny!

MITSOU (*scared*): Robert, what's wrong?

ROBERT: Nothing. I was just thinking of the sort of people who believe that ivy grows on battlefields. Don't be cross, Mitsou dear. In two hours I'll be here with a taxi.

MITSOU (*clumsily*): You needn't. I'll have the car——

ROBERT (*interrupting*): Then give it to the poor, or go
    home in it all by yourself. I shall be here, and I
    shall have a taxi.

He lifts his officer's cap, kisses her hand as though
she was not holding up her mouth, and watches her as
she goes. She runs, pushing her head forward like a
shop-girl who is late. She doesn't turn her head, but it
is only because she is afraid to see in the dreary light of
the bluish lamps the sombre face of a discontented,
ungrateful young man, whose mouth is still shining
from a last fierce kiss.

VII

Mᴵᵀˢᴼᵁ's flat. She comes in, in front of Robert. He is blinking in the electric light and walks forward in a rather hostile way, cautiously circling round the furniture. Mitsou turns round to look at him. She threw herself so wildly into the taxi he had waiting, the journey seemed so short (some sloppy kisses, some stiff remarks—"Was there a big audience? Not too tired?" "What on earth did you do for those two hours?" and so on) that she hasn't had time to find out if "he's still quarrelling" as she thinks of it, childishly. No, he isn't quarrelling, but he is watchful. He is watching those strange doors, and the chandelier of the Goths—in short the whole room whose luxury just because it is so commonplace reminds him of the provinces, with their lace and scollops and thick carpets. There is the astounding bed waiting for them. A marital bed, whose sheets are a little coarse, whose pillows have blue bows on them, and whose silk counterpane is quilted. A big bed, for sleeping in and for conceiving children in. "If I go anywhere near that bed," Robert thinks, "I'm finished." For he has just noticed that he is falling asleep on his feet.

MITSOU: We can talk comfortably now, dear; there's no one here. Come and let me show you. This is the bathroom; I'll run a bath right away. (*He hears the*

taps run, and smiles a comfortable smile. He has already
had one bath this morning; he would have as many more
as you liked): This is the boudoir. That way you go
out into the passage and that is the doubleyou.
Come here and I'll show you how the light turns
on in it.

ROBERT (*with male shyness*): Never mind, Mitsou. I'll
find it.

MITSOU: That's what people say, and then in the night
you want to get up to weewee and you bang into
everything and land up in the kitchen. Now just
look, the switch is to the left of the door. Does
it annoy you to be shown the doubleyou?
Gracious, you are a difficult person. You don't
ever mind asking for a drink and then you won't
talk about what everyone needs when they've had
a drink. Now, this is the sitting-room.

Robert follows her and looks vaguely at the South
Sea Islands cushions and the fake Dresden china. He is
thinking only about the bed. Those huge fat pillows
that you slip your arm underneath to find a cool place.
The musical elasticity of the mattress. That white,
smooth plain, the sheet. To drop down on it, one leg
that way, one leg this, and fall asleep. "Asleep?" he
thinks with a start. "It wasn't to sleep that I came
here."

Mitsou has brought him back into the bedroom. In
her black frock, with her eyes chastely lowered and her

long, patrician neck, she looks as meek as a bride.
Robert is not touched by it, but all the same, in black
against a lace background, Mitsou is a charming
picture, and he smiles.

ROBERT: What are you thinking of, Mitsou?

MITSOU (*raising her eyes, modestly*): I was thinking I
would undress in the boudoir. The bath is full;
I'll only take ten minutes, then I'll run another
one for you and then——

ROBERT (*greedily, looking at the bed*): And then we'll go
to bed!

MITSOU (*flattered*): Darling! (*She throws her arms round
his neck, kisses him and runs off.*)

Robert, left alone, stands for a moment by the bed.
"Only my cheek," he says to himself. "Just to put my
cheek down on the pillow for a moment while I'm
waiting. Don't let's be a damned fool. If I once put my
face down on that white linen what Mitsou finds when
she comes back will be a wallowing beast in boots,
snoring away on the bed." He drops into an armchair
and tries to think about Mitsou. He falls at once into
the rigid sleep of a soldier, sitting up, head erect, face
stiff. This petrification covers a series of brief dreams,
in which war and boyhood (for him so close together)
mingle their memories. Blackening blood in great
pools, flashes of fire, a holiday house in the country, a
flat bottomed boat on the river in the sun. He is bare-
footed, a small boy again, scooping the water for

tadpoles with a straw hat, when Mitsou re-appears and wakes him.

MITSOU (*in a peach-coloured wrap, her hair hanging down, very moved, very brave.*) Here I am. I'm ready.

ROBERT (*delighted because she has no pyjamas on*): My darling! That's the phrase for a sacrifice.

He takes her in his arms, and becomes solemn again, because she is naked and because she is trembling.

ROBERT: Mitsou, I apologise for my unsuitable dress. May I go to the bathroom?

MITSOU (*very solemn too*): Yes. I've filled the bath. I think everything's there.

He goes off. He enjoys thoroughly the hot water, splashing with his feet in the bath, rubbing himself with soap and the bath glove, noting the earnest care with which Mitsou has provided a fresh soap tablet, new towels, bath salts, and scented toilet water. Meanwhile she is getting timidly into bed. She is trembling very slightly and watches the pink ribbon quiver on her silk wrap which she has kept on. She listens respectfully to the muffled noises coming from the bathroom. Suddenly she thinks of an evening last week when Fluff came leaping down the staircase of the Empyrée to keep a date, and was calling out quite shamelessly: "Cheers, girls! There's going to be lovemaking! There's going to be lovemaking!" (only she didn't use the word "lovemaking"). Mitsou doesn't feel like dancing or like shouting; she ruminates a

minute and then shakes her head: "Yes. But then, for
Fluff, it wasn't a love affair." Then she thinks, with a
sense of shame, of an earlier time, when she gave herself, with a cold politeness, to the Respectable Man,
whose embraces were no use to her. "What a long way
that seems! I don't know where I am. I shan't ever
know. . . . I am going to seem like an old maid." She
sighs.—Robert comes in without knocking. He is
wearing a bathrobe.

MITSOU (*sitting up straight on her bottom*): But I put
   pyjamas out for you! On the chair at the foot of
   the bath.

ROBERT (*completely revived by the bath*): Do you think
   I'd wear reach-me-downs?

He drops off the bathrobe and stands there naked,
certain of getting his effect. But it is pearls before
swine, for Mitsou thinks any man "a fine figure" who
hasn't got a paunch. She turns away her eyes, which
is a great pity, makes herself as small as she can on
her side of the bed, and says:

"You'll be sure to catch cold."

With one jump he is on the bed, opens it, dives in
and slips his left arm round Mitsou's waist. He pulls
her to him and presses her whole body against his.
She lets out a small squeal like an animal which has
been crushed and then stays dumbly squashed against
him, breathing very fast.

ROBERT (*victoriously*): Aha! Aha!

But it would be hard for him to say if his cry of victory is about his capture of Mitsou, or about the sheet. It is caressing all his body with the sweetness of the indescribable surface of hard linen, which he has so often remembered. Close to his own face there is another young face, with big eyes which are very dark in the half light, a fresh round face, with a disorder of hair around it. He is almost touching her nose, a very small nose, which makes kisses so easy. He is breathing a breath that still has a faint scent of toothpaste and of the toilet water with which she rubbed her cheeks. He uses his bare knees to separate two knees which are still protected by silk, and easily settles his leg between two smooth thighs. He can feel they are beautifully rounded, and the flesh is firm and resilient. He is very comfortably placed so. If he had the courage, he would say to this unknown young woman whom he is embracing so intimately: "Look, my dear, shall we stay just like this? Let's go to sleep, if we want to—or talk, but only a little. Or we can cuddle a little, but quite platonically, without any nonsense. We can do more if we feel like it. It's quite possible that desire will wake both of us up, some time during the night. . . . But unfortunately that delicate armistice isn't allowed. Because we each of us are afraid of failing the other I have got to pull up or open out that silky veil, which feels so very nice as a matter of fact. I have got to break up our friendly hug. I have got to bustle and you have got to hand yourself over. Sure enough we shall be happy afterwards, like children who break a window to get some fresh air. Afterwards they sometimes think the window had its use. Perhaps it was even better than a draught. Oh, well. Let's go!"

He doesn't only think that last phrase; he says it.

ROBERT: Let's go!

MITSOU (*vaguely worried*): Go where?

ROBERT (*compassionately, for she is really very pretty*): My dear, I am a pest. Let's go away from this still-ness, this playing at Paul and Virginie, and to hell with all figleaves!

MITSOU (*who is quite contented, just now, to have no idea what he is talking about*): Yes, of course.

But she closes her eyelids and her fingers stay as chaste as her eyes.

ROBERT: (*in a whisper*): Are you asleep, Mitsou?

MITSOU (*the same*): Fast asleep.

She looks under her eyelashes at this pretty, naked faun who is crouching over her. He laughs, because he has seen the black and white of her mischievous eyes; she answers with a nervous sharp laugh herself. The simple lovely gaiety of animals has come close to them; each is near to a friendly biting, rolling and struggling; but each too remembers the need for making love, that unavoidable embrace. "Let's go!"

He puts into it a hearty good will which his youth soon warms into something more; his lovemaking follows a standard path. Mouth first, yes; certainly the mouth. Now the throat, never forget the throat; it hardly fills his two hands, and is straight enough to deserve the lingering, idolatrous respect he pays it.

MITSOU (*excited, and almost crying*): Oh!

Her exclamation, the drooping curve of her mouth, and the hope that she might really cry, excite the invader more than he intended. He rushes through all the stages which the most elementary rules of lovemaking prescribe. In one leap, Robert has taken everything that his white victim has to offer; she is spread out underneath him with her hair streaming; she has made no resistance. He takes a moment to savour fully, motionless within, the pleasure of what he has seized. Then the slow rhythm begins, to the tune of an unheard dirge, the dance of two joined bodies which are linked together as if they were healing and closing a wound.

In Mitsou's bedroom, for the first time, there is a magnificent picture thrown upon the lace covered wall at the head of her bed: it is the shadow of the body of a naked rider, broad shouldered and narrow waisted, arched over his mount that you cannot see.

VIII

THREE o'clock in the morning. He is asleep. She
wakes up, perhaps because he has moved, perhaps because they forgot to turn the light out. She is a
little lost as she wakens, but in a moment she remembers; a young man is next to her, a young man who
became her lover about midnight, briefly and almost
silently, and then fell asleep next to her, as suddenly
as people fall dead.

She is tired but clear-eyed. She only remembers a
most unusual pleasure, the pleasure of holding close to
her a beautiful young body which smelt sweeter as it
grew warmer, like cedar wood when you rub it, and
which fitted into hers exactly, as closely as petals in a
bud; this way it was nice, and that way it was nicer,
and each time he changed it was better. It is that she is
grateful for, not for the sharp excitement, which she
doesn't value very much.

He is sleeping on his side, with one arm under his
head. She feels guilty at staring at him. If he was awake,
would he allow her to examine so carefully the veins
under his white skin, and the fuzz below his flat
nipples, which makes a fleur de lis on his breast?
There is a white scar on his shoulder. Two vaccination
marks on his upper arm. His ribs show their arched
shape through his skin; hasn't he got thinner and

paler in these last few weeks? Where has he been living and what has it been like? His fine hands are very dark, at the end of his white arms; trench digging, steel, fire—which is responsible for hardening them and breaking their nails?

Can Mitsou kiss that open hand without waking its serious sleeping owner? No, she can't; he has moved; he is still moving. He is dreaming. The skin of his forehead, his eyebrows, the quivering corners of his mouth, all his features are suddenly filled with a life which has nothing to do with everyday joy or sorrow. Something outside this world is tormenting this prisoner of a dream. Mitsou is horrified as he struggles and groans; his helpless feet attempt to run, and he tries in vain to get up. A sort of sob breaks up the agony in his unhappy face just at the moment that Mitsou has decided to call him back from his dreams and save him. He falls back into the serene sleep that has been momentarily disturbed by war, terror, carnage and death.

While her hand is still raised to wake him Mitsou leans over him and watches the last ripples of his dream vanish on her lover's face. A final twitch, a sudden flash of mother-of-pearl under his eyelids, and he is fast asleep again, freed from his anxious spirit. "You would think he had gone away", Mitsou considers. But she doesn't let the faint but unpleasant thought become too clear, the thought that she is watching her lover leave her on a ship, the ship of sleep.

She doesn't feel sleepy. The bed smells nice. She has never bent over the Respectable Man and watched him sleep. What is he like when he sleeps? She doesn't know. She thinks for a moment of that elegant fifty-year-old in blue pyjamas, her skin creeps, and she puts the picture aside. "It isn't suitable at all." But there's another picture behind it: the Respectable Man sitting in front of her at the lunch table at a quarter to one. "What shall I do?" Three o'clock in the morning; that means she has nine hours still. She turns her head unconsciously towards the window where the night is fading; the instinctive movement of prisoners or caged animals. "What shall I do?" Tell the truth; that was what she first thought of, because she is good, light-hearted, and rather simple even if she is very young. But she is not going to tell this truth without the per-mission of the man sleeping next to her there; her secret isn't only hers. There is a name that she is not going to tell to the Respectable Man, not out of vanity, nor unkindness, nor even sheer excess of joy; she will only tell because the right time has come to tell it— if it ever does. Mitsou shakes her head and her black ringlets, "No," she says to herself, "I mustn't say anything to Pierre. Until I'm told otherwise, it's more decent to lie about it. Robert is to decide. . . . If he doesn't decide anything, well——" She looks at him rather frightenedly. He is now in the land of the deepest sleep there is, where no dreams come, and he is as handsome as an embalmed body. "Is that man to be my life?" Mitsou prays. "Oh, if only he was willing. . . ." Immediately she rises to the heights of completely mundane heroism. "If only he was willing, I wouldn't need all these things I've got here. I'd just take one room somewhere. I'm earning seven hundred francs a month—eight hundred in the next revue. I'd sell my big diamond ring. I'd take cinema work like I did two years ago; he could come and fetch me after the theatre, when the war's over." She smiles, a swift ghost of a smile. "No. He wouldn't come. He wouldn't wait in my dressing-room. He wouldn't gossip with Fluff and Alice Weiss while I was on stage. He is too proud. He's difficult. He's not at all ordinary."

The sparrows are beginning to twitter, and Mitsou is tired of thinking. She yawns with cold and hunger; the discomfort of the morning is coming over her. She hasn't the energy to go and get the bananas, under-ripe cherries and dry biscuits four steps away. She tells herself she is utterly miserable and has no hope of ever going to sleep again; as she repeats this she lies back and fits herself against Robert's unmoving back, her knees in the crook of his half-folded legs, and falls fast asleep again.

Five o'clock. The sky that shows in the crack between the curtains is turning from blue to pink. Someone knocks against a piece of furniture in the house, or

shuts a door, and Robert suddenly answers it: "Yes?"
He sits straight up. He looks quickly round the room,
and then at the black head of the small wild animal
hidden in the white pillow—Mitsou asleep. He wakes
up like the twenty-year-old soldier he is—cheerful,
rested, aggressive, prepared to leap up and run to the
sun. But Mitsou stays asleep. "Poor child. She has slept
peacefully right through the night. And I . . . I didn't
disturb her." He starts to take her in his arms, and then
changes his mind. He waits to comb his hair with his
fingers and to rub his eyes; he drinks a little of the
tepid mineral water at the bedside table. He rebukes
himself for having slept "like a husband", and leans
over to her. Mitsou has vaguely noticed some movement round her, and moves away her arms that were
protecting her face. She is pale; the two crescents of
her eyelashes reflect the crescents of her eyebrows, as
the span of a bridge is repeated by another span in the
water of the river. Her mouth is tightly closed, small
and sad.

"How pretty she is," he notices. "And what a
pity . . ." He is almost thinking aloud, and has startled
himself. "What a pity what? Well . . . this is what. A
pity that when I saw her I stopped being in love with
Mitsou. In a minute or two I am going to prove to
her that she is beautiful and I am young and vigorous.
And that will have no importance. No importance at
all. All the same, I am sorry that it won't. There is a

trouble between me and Mitsou, something very inconvenient that is bothering me. It's perfectly all right that she should expect me to be unique, but I chose to want her too to be unusual. And it's so happened that she is. She's not like Germaine at Christmas or Lily in March, and not at all like—Good God, I'm forgetting already—like Cri-cri in September of last year."

He picks over a few quite agreeable memories and each time he comments loyally: "But Mitsou is better. Mitsou is better and all the same no affaire has ever left me so discontented. She's more affectionate than skilful in bed? That doesn't really matter. She's silly? No, she isn't. You're not silly if your sensibility is so good, and if your instinct tells you what you can't think out. Her real fault is . . ."

He lifts off a tiny curl which has fallen across Mitsou's cheek, and tries to get his case against her quite clear. "Her real fault is only this: she makes you have to think about her just when you want to say, 'You are only a little anxiety, you aren't big enough to be a real nuisance.' "

A ray of sunlight is reflected from a window across the street and makes a dancing square of light on the back of the window curtains; the young man is seized by a sort of animal impatience, an indistinct irritation, and a very distinct impulse to go away. "I could go away very easily," he thinks, looking at Mitsou, who is still asleep and is growing less pale as the light gets brighter. "There's nothing to stop me. Not her, she will let me go without any arguments or coquetry. She'll give me my freedom all right. But just at the moment I turn her off, there'll be a silent appeal, the camouflage of a very proud beggar: 'I don't want anything; I never asked you for anything, did I?'"

He realizes that whatever he does he looks like falling below Mitsou's level; he shrugs his shoulders and thinks, rather brutally, "Anyway, it's very pleasant."

The sight of Mitsou who hasn't moved brings back his natural kindness. "She is pretty," he repeats. "When she wakes up she'll say something silly. But Cri-cri in September poured out nonsense first thing in the morning, and so did Lily in March; and I forgave them at once. Or perhaps she will knock me out with one of her sentimental platitudes, as vast as the world and as stale. They upset me."

The strange room is getting lighter; he looks round it venomously.

"That statuette in soapy marble, the bowl hanging by chains from the ceiling, the Cupids pouring lace curtains down on to my head: I never expected anything like them. What did I expect to find, then? Well, a woman who wasn't Cri-cri or Lily. Or Mitsou. I'm twisting things. I'm exaggerating her negative virtues. I ought to say quite coarsely: 'She didn't amuse me; she didn't affect me enough to make me cry. The

motion of her narrow hips wasn't enough to give me
that violent pleasure that sends you wild. Or exhausts
you.' Then if that's so, all I have to do is to go away,
and add to Lily of some earlier month another entry:
'Mitsou in May.' No, it's not true. Something in this
girl is asking for what I can't and needn't give her,
because I'm young and a soldier. She seems to be
wanting, passionately, for me to help her to be like
the woman I shall love some day. She has a sort of
resemblance to her already. What has happened is that
a plough has turned up, much too soon, a sod where
there was the live seed, or rather the helpless and un-
formed larva, of the love of my future life. But I am
not going to drag my future love out of its eggshell,
not yet. It's not my fault that I've been living for three
years the sort of life where any action—or any refusal
to act—is forced to have an intense meaning, like a
religious problem. It's a kind of life when you are
forced to believe in the seriousness of everything, even
in the seriousness of not being in love. That's the real
reason, Mitsou, why I am in your bed trying to
evaluate the importance of our joint mistake, instead of
going away friendlily and then sending you postcards
from the trenches. I don't think it will kill you, will it,
to have had the light let in too soon on to your growing life? It won't. You will be a little upset, but you
will crawl back into your egg. I don't think it is for
me to bring you out of it. That is almost certainly

reserved for someone much more mature, more patient, more frivolous and more meticulous than I am. And he mustn't be stopped short as I am by the 'civvy' tone of all your words and thoughts. A lot of people know nothing at all about the life of young soldiers—frightened, inspired, sceptical, resigned, greedy but deprived of everything, weighed down by a sour and premature old age, borne up by childish confidence—and they don't know either how that civvy flavour spoils our occasional reappearances for a moment in our old life in our homes and towns, and with our women.

"Anyway, Mitsou my dear, you have made me think about the woman I'll love some day. I think she will have your sweetness, and a sort of pride like yours that will make her able to bear disappointments. I hope that as a dividend she'll also have a big heart behind similar small breasts, rather low-slung. I like to think, already, that she and I will speak the same language and we shan't be the least surprised when we meet each other."

He listens to his own thoughts, a little saddened at the sort of loneliness that is going to be his life until he finds the final edition of a Mitsou. In the streets a water hose crashes a jet of water on to the pavement. Empty milk churns are making a noise like Swiss cowbells. The naked young man makes up his mind, with his favourite word: "Let's go!" He leans over Mitsou, who is still asleep. "Goodbye, my darling", he says very softly before he wakes her. Then he does wake her, by pulling her close to him, kissing her, and saying in a loud, cheerful voice:

"Good morning, Mitsou!"

IX

THE same day, three o'clock in the afternoon. Mitsou has had lunch with the Respectable Man, and the Respectable Man noticed no change in her. She has learned now to keep a secret, and how to tell suitable lies, and how to keep her mouth shut to avoid lying; she is offering up these wretched concessions to convention as a sacrifice to her favourite love. The Respectable Man has just gone and has left with Mitsou the reassuring promise that he won't come to see her again until the same time tomorrow. Left to herself, Mitsou very nearly gave way for the first time in her life to a violent excitement, violent enough to make her smash a vase deliberately, jump with both feet on the silk seat of the armchair, throw cushions at the ceiling, or just make silly squalling noises. The Respectable Man has gone half an hour earlier than usual, and she has thirty minutes extra to get her face, her hair and her little body ready: Robert is going to call for her at five and they are going to drive in a taxi to the Bois de Boulogne, right to the empty avenues of Auteuil. When Robert left her she was tired, and a little disappointed because he wouldn't wait till the maid came and brought breakfast. But their kiss as he left had been a long one, and more loving than she had hoped for.

"When he said 'You're adorable' as he went,"
Mitsou said to herself, "I almost thought he was going
to say 'I love you.'" The memory is too delicious for
her even to smile at it, and so her seriousness is not
even shaken when the bell rings, and she says to herself,
with a certainty so absolute that for the minute it is
almost a comfort: "That's a letter. He isn't coming."

THE MAID (*coming in*): A letter brought by hand, ma'am.

MITSOU (*in a small voice*): Are they waiting for an answer?

THE MAID: No, ma'am. It was a soldier, a private. He
     didn't stay.

MITSOU: All right. Thank you.

She doesn't open the letter at once. She has to rest
for a minute, because she has felt a sudden, wholly
physical faintness, the kind that comes over you after
a violent nose-bleeding or a slight heart-attack. "How
very odd," she thinks, "it's like my heart turning
pale." Then she sits down by the window, opens the
letter, and reads it:

"Mitsou, my dear,—The captain with whom I came
on this special service has to go back tonight."

Mitsou stops and draws a long breath after that
sentence. She says to herself: "I understand. It isn't as
though he was cross with me, or had something at the
back of his mind." She even smiles, so as to prove to
herself that everything is all right, and, damn it all,
"there's a war on".

"Mitsou, my dear,—The captain with whom I came

on this special service has to go back tonight. Needless to say, dear Mitsou, I have to go too. His legs are covered in serge and leather; it is like an over-filled valise—not the sort of thighs I hoped to have next to mine tonight. I am rather afraid, my warm and smooth darling, to tell you just how much and in what way I am missing you. (Look, I have thoughtlessly gone back to calling you *vous* as we did in our letters, even though this morning we called each other *tu* with all our heart, and all our body too.) I should tell it you badly, and I don't really want to tell you. Remember it was only a little while ago you called me your 'twin', as if I was a classmate and a rival. Your infatuated rival then, darling, is not going to tell you what he misses most in leaving you, or what he misses least. It would swell your head, and also prick your little-girl vanity.

"The best thing for you to do when you've read this letter, Mitsou, is to sit down at that old pink desk which I saw in your boudoir and write me a letter. That way, I shan't have to wait too long for your first letter at the front. Tell me quite brutally if you are sulking over our lost afternoon, our dinner that has been postponed and our night together that we shall have some other time. Tell me too which you'd have chosen, if you'd been forced to have one or the other— the long drive with me or the short night, which would start so late and end so soon? I hadn't an opportunity, this time, to ask you the questions that can't be ignored

or evaded, when two mouths are close together, and
the whole of one body is cross-examining another.
I've not ravished a single one of your secrets. I'm still
under the pleasant slack influence of my old habit of
waiting a long time—it was always four days—for one
of your veils to fall and one of your phrases to come
through. Our conversation was made so slow by the
past that I began to associate you with an idea of
languidness and indifference. I lost that delusion last
night, in your arms. There could be no mistake; you
had your own rhythm and it drove me on, saying
'quicker, quicker still'.

"I don't know when I'll come back. I don't know if
I'll come back at all. Don't be upset, my dear; I only
mean by that that the roads are dreadful and a car accident may break my leg, and that bad drinking water
has given several men in my regiment dysentery. The
other thing, what you call 'danger', we just don't talk
about, that's all. The chief point is: You've got to
write to me, Mitsou. Perhaps it is cynical of me, but I
must admit to you I want to compare two Mitsous
that I know and have pressed against my breast:
Mitsou on paper and Mitsou on a bed. Here is another
admission, equally unwise: Supposing you get tired
of me before you see me again, and supposing you go
out a few weeks from now with another lieutenant,
dressed in blue and in love with Mitsou, as all French
lieutenants ought to be and would like to be, I think

I deserve a letter about it. A last letter from Mitsou full of her dangerous simplicity, her unanswerable sincerity, and her arguments which are always based only on the facts.

"I'm joking, Mitsou. It's a stupidly correct thing to do at the end of a letter, when you'd really rather complain and curse. I kiss your hands only, my dear; I am putting out of my mind for the minute, like a good boy, the memory of all the rest of your body that was so kind to me.

"Your

"Blue Lieutenant"

Mitsou to the Blue Lieutenant

I AM sitting at my little desk. But I didn't sit down at it at once, and I haven't started writing my letter to you without thinking about it, as you told me to. First of all it isn't my nature to, and I couldn't anyway. And next, a person has to have time to read a letter, to read it properly, and laugh and blow her nose, and wipe her eyes and think about it. I told you already. I can't write quickly. And anyway you didn't yourself write your own letter quickly. You took an awful long time about it for an officer who's been called back to duty. Darling, that isn't a reproach; don't bring your eyebrows together over your nose. It isn't a reproach and all the same it is. I'm wondering if I wouldn't

rather you'd written: "Am compelled to go back with
the captain. Love and kisses." Like a telegram, you
know. Please don't be cross; let me tell you first what
isn't all right and the nicer things will come later. Well,
there it is, you're going and it's horrid and it's even
worse than that. Now why make excuses for yourself
over it. I've got the idea that the excuses aren't so
much because you're going but because you're leaving
me. Now you'll be saying, "There's Mitsou again;
how can I go without also leaving her?" Well, of
course. It's difficult to explain, but it's not difficult to
understand. . . . Darling, only get one thing into your
head—I love you. Oh, I don't think I'm giving you a
nice present in saying that, quite the contrary. You
poor boy, I love you; that's more like. And if you
choose you can say when you read it, "That's very
nice for me, I don't think". A woman who loves you,
even a stupid woman like I, becomes an awful nuisance, she knows things and she guesses things. She's
like the electric light when you turn it on; one minute
there's only a switch and a stupid glass bulb, and the
next there's a sort of line of fire that lights everything up.

The nice part for you of this boring thing that is
happening to you is this, that now I know you can
count on me. Count on me for anything. To wait if
you want me to wait, and to guess it if there's something you're ashamed to tell me. Count on me too if
the idea comes to you to say to my face "it's all over

between us"; I'll show I know how to behave and you won't need any soft soap or the other thing.

And another thing, if you think I ought to change my job, or get myself more educated, or alter in some way or other, I can do that too, even if it's only to amuse you or to have something to talk to me of.

Does that make you feel a bit more comfortable about me loving you? Oh, I do hope it does. I'm more or less comforted on my side, because there's nothing I don't see, and your letter doesn't hide anything, least of all. Dear blue lieutenant, it isn't at all difficult to see that though you don't know it what you are really trying to do is to jump backwards to before our meeting yesterday. Nobody could say nicer things than you do about the letters we wrote each other before. A person who wasn't well brought up would just have said to me: "I was crazy about you until I met you. So let's wipe out the last twenty-four hours and start again." But the only use of being well brought up is that you can serve out nicely on a plate what other people throw in people's faces.

"There you are," you'll be saying, "there's that Mitsou being cross." Not cross or miserable, dear, and I do really believe I'm more comfortable in my mind than I was this morning. Think, I was asking myself then when I was all by myself "There's nobody who'll tell me what he really thinks of me" and of course I didn't expect to get that information from you. In your world nobody says "You're a thoroughly nasty woman, Miss". You say: "Madame, I am charmed to be with you. I must just slip out to get some cigarettes; I won't be a minute", and you leave her there for the rest of her life. I am not a thoroughly nasty woman, but I was afraid I mightn't ever see you again, not even in a letter.

As it is, after the first shock, I can see that there isn't much harm done. "Well," I say to myself, "he is writing to me. He remembers who I am, he asks me questions, he wants to know about me." You shall know everything, dear. Ask anything you want to. Which would I have preferred—the daytime drive or the night we were to have together? I haven't any doubt: I'd have chosen the night. My dear, a night together is less embarrassing, it's even less intimate. I shall always feel more or less good enough for you, provided I've got no clothes on and am lying in bed in your arms. The awful thing is that some time one's got to get up, and then I'm frightened of you. All that you looked for in me while we were together and didn't get—I got all that from you. I'm still being surprised at your skin being so nice, and the solemn expression that you have when you're asleep, and the way you sleep without night clothes. I didn't think your feet would be so small. And I thought too that as you were so refined a young man and ate so elegantly in the restaurant and had all sorts of special ways,

I thought that you would go in for a lot of elaboration
in making love. But not at all. All you were interested
in was in taking me at once, smoothly and thoroughly,
and I was delighted. So how can you expect I shouldn't
be in love with you?

The difficult thing for you, dear, would be to stop
me loving you. What's almost impossible for me, is
to get you to love me. I'm saying "almost", because
I'm the sort of person who won't believe in the worst
sort of disasters, or of good luck. "Mitsou's much too
sensible for her age", the girls used to say. If I hadn't
been, I wouldn't of thought things out so carefully
while you were asleep, last night. While you were
sleeping, darling, I gave up all hope of the very best
you might have given me. But I was being like a fire
brigade, when it tries to save just a little part of a
building. You see I am being quite humble, but I'm
not begging for anything; please don't think that. If
you answer me by saying "Goodbye, Mitsou", it
won't kill me. I have a tough little heart, and it can
flourish on disappointment. I am rather like Gitanette,
you know; they try to comfort her all the time because
of a great sorrow and she answers: "What good would
it do me not to have a disappointment to brood over?
What'd I do with myself?"

Meanwhile even if I am pigheaded I am going on
hoping that you won't leave behind just a disappointment. When you found me I was behind the footlights

singing a song which had only three verses, and I didn't have even three ideas in my head. Whatever you liked in me, it was you who planted it there; anyway, whoever did, it struck root all right. Weren't you surprised how I'd grown after only two months? The trouble was that as soon as I actually saw you all my petals curled up. Still, all the same, a woman who's in love does grow fast. She blooms; she finds out how to put on an elegance and a colour that will fool even the smartest people. My dear, I will try to fool you. This is a tremendous ambition, and anyway you never asked me to go for a walk with you that would go on all our lives, dear Blue Lieutenant. But let's begin with the easiest bit first. Please make me a present by sleeping with me again; let me have the surprise of following you so easily to the moment of delight. Let me have the trust and friendliness of your body; perhaps one night, groping and hardly noticed, those two things may bring me myself to you.

Mitsou

MUSIC-HALL SIDELIGHTS

Translated by
ANNE-MARIE CALLIMACHI

CONTENTS

ON TOUR

THE HALT

HERE we are at Flers. . . . A bumpy, sluggish train has just deposited our sleepy troupe and abandoned us, yawning and disgruntled, on a fine spring afternoon, the air sharpened by a breeze blowing from the east, across a blue sky streaked with light cloud and scented with lilac just bursting into bloom.

Its freshness stings our cheeks, and we screw up our smarting eyes like convalescents prematurely allowed out. We have a two-and-a-half-hour wait before the train that is to take us on.

"Two and a half hours! What shall we do with ourselves?"

"We can send off picture postcards. . . ."

"We can have some coffee. . . ."

"We might play a game of piquet. . . ."

"We could look at the town. . . ."

The manager of our Touring Company suggests a visit to the Park. That will give him time for forty winks in the buffet, nose buried in his turned-up collar, heedless of his peevish flock bleating around him.

"Let's go and see the Park!"

Now we are outside the station, and the hostile curiosity of this small town escorts us on our way.

"These people here have never seen a thing," mutters the ingénue, in aggressive mood. "Anyhow, the towns where we don't perform are always filled with 'bystanders'."

"And so are those where we do," observes the disillusioned duenna.

We are an ugly lot, graceless and lacking humility: pale from too hard work, or flushed after a hastily snatched lunch. The rain at Douai, the sun at Nîmes, the salty breezes at Biarritz have added a green or rusty tarnish to our lamentable touring 'outer garments', ample misery-hiding cloaks which still pretentiously boast an "English style". Trailing over the length and breadth of France, we have slept in our crumpled bonnets, all of us except the *grande coquette*, above whose head wave pompously—stuck on the top of a dusty black velvet tray —three funereal ostrich plumes.

Today I gaze at these three feathers as if I had never seen them before; they look fit to adorn a hearse, and so does the woman beneath them.

She seems out of keeping in the "town where we don't perform", rather ludicrous, with her Bourbon profile and her recurrent "I don't know why everyone tells me I resemble Sarah! What do you think?"

A gay little squall tugs at our skirts as we turn the corner into a square, and the carefully waved tresses of the ingénue's peroxide hair stream out in the wind. She utters a shriek as she clutches her hat, and I can see across her forehead—between eyebrows and hair—a carelessly removed red line, the trace of last night's make up!

Why have I not the strength to look away when the duenna's bloomers brave the light of day! They are tan-coloured bloomers and fall in folds over her cloth booties! No mirage could distract my attention from the male star's shirt collar, greyish white, with a thin streak of "ochre foundation" along the neck-line. No enchanted drop-curtain of flowers and tremulous leafage could make me overlook the comic's pipe, that fat, old, juicy pipe; the fag-end stuck to the under-manager's lip; the purple ribbon, turning black, in the make-up man's button-hole; the senior lead's matted beard, ill-dyed and in part dis-coloured! They are all so crudely conspicuous in "the town where we don't perform"!

But what about myself? Alas, what made me dawdle in front of the watchmaker's shop, allowing the mirror there time to show me my shimmerless hair, the sad twin-shadows under my eyes, lips parched with thirst, and my flabby figure in a chestnut-brown tailor-made whose limp flaps rise and fall with every step I take! I look like a discouraged beetle, battered by the rains of a spring night. I look like a moulting bird. I look like a governess in distress. I look . . . Good Lord, I look like an actress on tour, and that speaks for itself

At last, the promised Park! The reward justifies our long walk, dragging our tired feet, exhausted from keep-ing on our boots for eighteen hours a day. A deep, shady park; a slumbering castle, its shutters closed, set in the midst of a lawn; avenues of trees, just beginning to unfurl their sparse tender foliage; bluebells and cowslips studding the grass.

How can one help shivering with delight when one's hot fingers close round the stem of a live flower, cool from the shade and stiff with new born vigour! The filtered light, kind to raddled faces, imposes a relaxed silence. Suddenly a gust of keen air falls from the tree-tops, dashes off down the alley chasing stray twigs, then vanishes in front of us, like an impish ghost.

We are tongue-tied, not for long enough.

"Oh, the countryside!" sighs the ingénue.

"Yes. If only one could sit down," suggests the duenna, "my legs are pressing into my body."

At the foot of a satin-boled beech we take a rest, inglorious and unattractive strollers. The men smoke; the women turn their eyes toward the blue perspectives of the alley, toward a blazing bush of rhododendrons, the colour of red-hot embers, spreading over a neighbouring lawn.

"For my part, the country just drains me . . ." says the comic with an unconcealed yawn, "makes me damned sleepy!"

"Yes, but it's healthy tiredness," decrees the pompous duenna.

The ingénue shrugs her plump shoulders: "Healthy tiredness! You make me sweat! Nothing ages a woman like living in the country, it's a well-known fact."

Slowly the under-manager extracts his pipe from his mouth, spits, then starts quoting: "*A melancholy feeling, not devoid of grandeur, surges from . . .*"

"Oh, shut up!" grumbles the *jeune premier*, consulting his watch as if terrified of missing a stage-entrance.

A lanky boy, tall and pale-faced, who plays odd-job parts, is watching the movements of a little "dung-beetle" with steel-blue armour, teasing it with a long straw.

I take deep, exhaustive breaths, trying to detect and recapture forgotten smells that are wafted to me as from the depths of a clear well. Some elude me, and I am unable to remember their names.

None of us laughs, and if the *grande coquette* hums softly to herself, it is bound to be a broken, soleful little tune. We don't feel at ease here: we are surrounded by too much beauty.

At the end of the avenue a friendly peacock appears, and behind his wide-spread fan we notice that the sky is turning pink. Evening is upon us. Slowly the peacock advances in our direction, like a courteous park-keeper whose task it is to evict us. Oh, surely, we must fly! My companions are by now almost on the run.

"What if we missed it, children!"

We all know well enough that we shall not miss our train. But we are fleeing the beautiful garden, its silence and its peace, the lovely leisure, the solitude of which we are unworthy. We hurry towards the hotel, to the stifling dressing-rooms, the blinding footlights. We scurry along, pressed for time, talkative, screeching like chickens, hurrying towards the illusion of living at high speed, of keeping warm, working hard, shunning thought, and refusing to be burdened with regrets, remorse or memories.

ARRIVAL AND REHEARSAL

TOWARDS eleven o'clock we arrive at X, a large town (whose name is of no consequence), where we are fairly well paid and have to work hard; the pampered audiences demand "Star Numbers" straight from Paris. It is raining, one of those mild spring showers that induce drowsiness and reduce one's calves to pulp.

The heavy lunch and the smoky atmosphere of the tavern, after a long night on the train, have turned me into a sulky little creature, reluctant to face the afternoon's work. But Brague stands no trifling.

"Shuffle your guts, come on. The rehearsal's at two sharp."

"Bother! I'm going back to the hotel to get some sleep! Besides, I don't like you addressing me in that tone of voice."

"Apologies, Princess. I simply wanted to beg you to have the extreme kindness of stirring up your wits. Fresh plasters await us!"

"What plasters?"

"Those of the 'Establishment'. We're opening cold tonight."

I had forgotten. This evening we are to inaugurate a brand new music-hall, called the "Atlantic", or the "Gigantic", or the "Olympic"—in any case, the name of a liner. Three thousands seats, an American Bar, attractions in the outer-galleries during the intervals, and a gipsy band in the main hall! We'll read about all these glories in tomorrow's papers. In the meantime it makes no difference to us, except that we are certain to cough in the dressing-rooms, since new central heating never works, making the place either too hot or not warm enough.

I meekly follow Brague, who elbows his way along the North Avenue, cluttered with clerks and shopgirls, hurrying, like ourselves, to their factories. A nipping March sun makes the rainy air smoke, and my damp hair hangs limp, as in a steam bath. Brague's too long overcoat flaps over his heels, gathering mud at each step. Taken at our face-value we are just worth ten francs per evening: Brague, speckled with dirt; myself drunk with sleep, sporting a Skye-terrier's hair-do!

I let my companion guide me and, half dozing, I run over in my mind a few comforting facts and figures. The rehearsal is fixed for two o'clock sharp; with delays, we can count on half past four. One-and-a-half to two hours' work with the orchestra and we should be back at the hotel about seven o'clock, there to dress, and dine,

and return to the joint by nine; by a quarter to twelve
I'll be in my own clothes again and just in time for a
lemonade in the tavern. Well! Let's be reasonable and
hope, God willing, that within ten little hours I shall
once again be in a bed, with the right to sleep in it until
lunch-time the next day! A bed, a nice fresh bed, with
smoothly drawn sheets and a hot water bottle at the end
of it, soft to the feet like a live animal's tummy.

Brague turns left—I turn left; he stops short—I stop
short.

"Good Lord!" he exclaims, "it isn't possible!"

Wide awake, I too judge at a glance that it really is not
possible.

Huge dust-carts, laden with sacks of plaster, obstruct
the street. Scaffolding screens a light coloured building
that looks blurred and barely condensed into shape, on
which masons are hastily moulding laurel wreaths,
naked females and Louis XVI garlands above a dark
porch. Beyond this can be heard a tumult of inarticulate
shouts, a battery of hammers, the screeching of saws, as
though the whole assembly of the Niebelungen were
busy at their forges.

"Is that it?"

"That is it."

"Are you certain, Brague?"

In reply I receive a fulminating glance, that should have
been reserved solely for the Olympic's improvident
architect.

"I just meant, you're certain we rehearse here?"

The rehearsal takes place. It passes all comprehension,
but the rehearsal takes place. We go on through the dark
porch under a sticky shower of liquid plaster; we jump
over rolls of carpet in the process of being laid, its royal
purple already bearing marks of muddy soles. We climb

a temporary ladder leading, behind the stage floor, to the artistes' dressing-rooms, and finally we emerge, scared and deafened, in front of the orchestra.

About thirty performers are disporting themselves here. Bursts of music reach us during lulls in the hammering. In the conductor's rostrum a lean, hairy, bearded human being beats time with arms, hands and head, his eyes turned upward to the friezes with the ecstatic serenity of a deaf mute.

There we are, a good fifteen "Numbers", bewildered, and already discouraged. We have never met before, yet we recognise each other. Here is the *diseur*, paid eight francs a night, who doesn't care a hoot what goes on.

"I don't care a d——. I'm engaged as from this evening, and cash-in as from this evening."

There is the comic, with a face like a sneaky solicitor's clerk, who talks of "going to law", and foresees "a very interesting case".

There is the German family, athletes of the flying trapeze, seven Herculean figures with childish features, affrighted, amazed, already worried by the fear of being thrown out of work.

There stands the little "songstress", who's always "out of luck", the one who's always in "trouble with the management", and is supposed to have been robbed of "twenty thousand francs-worth of jewellery" last month, Marseilles! Naturally she is also the one who's lost her costumes' trunk on her way here and has had "words" with the proprietor of her hotel.

There is even, out in front, an extraordinary little man, looking worn, his cheeks furrowed by two deep ravines, a "star tenor" in his fifties, grown old in goodness knows what outlandish places. Indifferent to the noise, he rehearses implacably.

Every other minute he flings his arms wide to stop the orchestra, rushing from the double-bass to the kettle-drums, bent in two over the footlights. He looks like a stormy petrel riding the tempest. When he sings, he emits long shrill notes, metallic and malevolent, in an attempt to bring to life an obsolete repertory in which he impersonates, in turn, Pedro the Bandit, the light-hearted cavalier who forsakes Manon, the crazed villain and his sinister cackling at night on the moors. He scares me, but delights Brague, who instinctively reverts to his nomad fatalism.

Risking his luck in the general confusion, my companion lights the forbidden "fag" and lends an amused ear to the "vocal phenomenon", a dark lady who spins out almost inaudible high C's.

"She's killing, isn't she? Makes me feel as if I were listening through the wrong end of my opera-glasses."

His laughter is infectious. Mysteriously a comforting cheerfulness starts to spread among us. We feel the approach of night, of the hour when the lamps are lit, the hour of our real awakening, of our glory.

"*ANANKE!*" suddenly shouts the litigious comic, a high-brow in his way. "If we perform, we perform; and if we don't . . . well we don't."

With a ballet-dancer's leap he skims over the edge of the stage-box, ready to give the electricians a helpful hand. The "out-of-luck" girl goes to crack an acid drop with the Herculean septet. My drowsiness has left me and I settle down on a roll of linoleum, side by side with the "vocal phenomenon" who is all set to tell my fortune! Still another carefree hour ahead, empty of thought or plans.

Happy in our obtuse way, devoid of intuition or fore-sight, we give no thought to the future, to misfortune, to old age—or to the impending failure of this altogether too new and luxurious "Establishment" which is due to go smash one month from today, precisely on "Saint-Pay-Day".

A BAD MORNING

NOT one of us four feels fit to face the harsh light that falls from the glass roof like a vertical cold shower. It is nine in the morning; that is, dawn for the likes of us who go to bed late. Is it really possible that there can still exist, within a mile or so, a warm bed and a breakfast cup still steaming with the dregs of scented tea? I feel as if I shall never again lay myself down in my bed. I find this rehearsal room, the scene of our reluctant and too early foregatherings, utterly depressing.

"Aah . . ." the lovely Bastienne yawns expressively.

Brague, the mimic, throws her a fearsome glance, as much as to say, "Serves you right". He is pale and ill-shaven, whereas the lovely Bastienne, battered and shrunk to nothing inside her sentry-box of a coat, would wring the heart of anyone other than a good companion, by the pink swellings under her eyes and her bloodless ears. Palestrier, the composer, his nose bright purple on a wan countenance, is the personification of a drunk who has spent the night unconscious in a police-station. As for myself! Good God, a sabre slash across one cheek, limp skeins of hair, and skin left dry by my lazy bloodstream! One might think we are showing off, exaggerating our disgrace, in a fit of witless sadism. "Serves you right", say Brague's eyes, probing my sunken cheeks; while mine retort, "You're just such another wreck yourself."

Instead of shortening the rehearsal of our mime, we

fritter time away. Palestrier starts on a salacious story, which could be funny, were it not that the dead cigarette he keeps masticating imparts a most obnoxious smell to his every word. The stove roars yet does not heat the hall, and we peer into its small mica-window, like chilled savages hoping for some miraculous sunrise.

"What do they burn in it, I wonder?" Palestrier hazards. "Newspaper logs, maybe, bound together with wire thread. I know how to make that stuff. I learned how from an old lady, the year I won my prize at the *Conservatoire*. She used to cough up three francs to make me play waltzes for her. There were times when I'd turn up, and she's just say 'We'll have no music today; my little bitch is nervy, and the piano puts her on edge!' So she would invite me to help with the fuel provision— nothing but newspapers and wire. It was she, too, who taught me how to burnish brass. I certainly didn't waste my time with her. In those days, providing I could feed, I would have clipped dogs and doctored cats!"

In the now glowing square of mica he gazes at the vision of his needy youth, the period when his talent struggled within him like a splendid, famished beast. As he sits staring, his pale-faced hungry youth becomes so alive that he reverts to the juicy slang of the suburbs, the drawling accent and thick voice; and, sticking both hands in his pockets, he allows a shudder to shake his frame.

On this harsh winter morning we lack courage, lack all incentive to face the future. There is nothing inside us to burst into flame or blossom amid the dirty snow. Crouched and fearful, we are driven back by the hour, the cold, our rude awakening, the momentary malevolence in the air, to the most miserable, most humiliating moments of our past.

"The same goes for me," Brague breaks out suddenly. "Just to be able to eat one's fill. . . . People who've always had plenty can't imagine what that means. I remember a time when I still had some credit at the pub, but never a chance to make any dough. When I drank down my glass of red wine . . . well, I could have cried just at the thought of a fresh little crust to dip into it."

"The same goes for me . . ." the lovely Bastienne takes her cue. "When I was a mere kid—fifteen or sixteen—I'd all but faint in the mornings at the dancing-class, because I hadn't had enough to eat; but if the ballet-mistress asked me whether I was ill, I'd brag and answer: 'It's my lover, Madame, he's exhausted me.' A lover indeed! As if I'd even known what it meant to have one! She'd throw her arms in the air: 'Ah, you won't keep your queenly beauty for long! But what on earth have you all got in those bodies of yours?' What I had *not* got in my body was a good plateful of soup, and that's a cert."

She speaks slowly, with assiduous care, as if she were spelling out her reminiscences. Sitting with her knees wide apart, the lovely Bastienne has sunk into the posture of a housewife watching her pot boil. Her "queenly beauty" and her brassy smile have been discarded as if they were mere stage props.

A few slammed chords, a run up the scale by stumbling numb fingers, excite a superficial thrill. I shall have to move out of the posture of a hibernating animal, head inclined on one shoulder, hands tightly clasped like cold-stricken paws. I was not asleep. I am only, like my companions, emerging from a bitter dream. Hunger, thirst . . . they should be a full-time torture, simple and complete, leaving no room for other torments. Privation prevents all thought, and substitutes for any other mental image that of a hot sweet-smelling dish, and reduces hope to the shape of a rounded loaf set in rays of glory.

Brague is the first to jump to his feet. Rough and ready advice and inevitable invective assume, as they flow from his lips, a most familiar sound. What a string of ugly words to accompany so graceful an action! How many traces of trial and error are to be seen on the faces of the three mimes, where effort sets a too quickly broken mask! Hands that we compel to speak our lines, arms for an instant eloquent, seem suddenly to be shattered, and by their strengthless collapse transform us into mutilated statues.

No matter. Our goal, though difficult to attain, is not inaccessible. Words, as we cease to feel their urgency, become detached from us, like graceless vein-stones from a precious gem. Invested with a subtler task than those who speak classical verse or exchange witticisms in lively prose, we are eager to banish from our mute dialogues the earthbound word, the one obstacle between us and silence—perfect, limpid, rhythmic silence—proud to give expression to every emotion and every feeling, and accepting no other support, no other restraint than that of Music.

THE CIRCUS HORSE

"Dressing-room 17, shall I find it along here?"

" . . . "

"Thank you very much, Madame. Coming straight in out of the street, one is quite dazed by the darkness of this corridor. . . . So, as things are, it looks like our being neighbours!"

" . . . "

"True, it's nothing to write home about, but I've seen worse, as artistes' dressing-rooms go. Oh! please, don't bother, I can drag it alone; it's my costumes' trunk. Anyway my husband won't be long now: he's engaged at present in speaking to the management. You've turned your dressing-room into something quite pretty, Madame. Ah! and there's your poster. I caught sight of it on the walls on our way from the station. A full length poster, and in three colours, that always spells class. So you're the lady with the detective dogs?"

" . . . "

"Oh, sorry, I was cònfusing you. Pantomine, that's it, and very interesting too. It was actually in that line I first worked, before I took up the weights! Come to think of it, I had a little pink apron with pockets, and patent-leather shoes, something after the *soubrette* style, you know. Pantomime's not much of a bind, when all's said and done. One hand on your heart, a finger to your lips, which goes for "I love you", and then you take your bow, that's all there is to it! But I very soon got married, and off I went, to serious work!

" . . . "

"Yes, weights are my job. I don't look the part? Because I'm so small, you mean? That's just what deceives people, but you'll see for yourself tonight. We're billed as 'Ida and Hector', you've heard of us, surely? We've just done Marseilles and Lyons, on our way up from Tunis."

" . . . !"

"Lucky? Because we've done a fortnight in Tunis? I don't see what's so lucky about that. Far rather play Marseilles and Lyons, or even Saint-Etienne. Hamburg! There's a proper town for you! Naturally I'm not talking of big capitals, like Berlin or Vienna, places one can call big cities, specially when it comes to real slap-up establishments."

" . . . ?"

"Why, of course, we've moved around, gone places! You make me laugh, speaking so envious-like! As far as travelling goes, I'd willingly let you have my share, and no tears shed!"

" . . . ?"

"Not that I've had enough of it, but that I've just never cared for travel. I'm the cosy sort. So's my husband, Hector. But, you see, there's just the two of us in our show and the best we can hope for is three weeks in the same town, or a month at most, in spite of our number being very good to look at, very well presented. Hector with his athletics, all very flexible and light, and me with my weights, and a very special whirl-wind waltz, very new, very stylish, to finish off our number. So—what more d'you want? We get around quite a bit, the way things go!"

" . . . !"

"It's Tunis that gets you, that's clear enough! And I wonder why, considering the establishment there's no great shakes!"

" . . . !"

"Oh, it's to see the town? and the surroundings too? Well, if that's your idea, I'm hardly the one to inform you; I've not seen much of it."

" . . . ?"

"Yes, I've been a little bit here, a little bit there. It's a big enough town. There are lots of Arabs. Then there are the small booths—*souks* they call them—along the covered streets; but they're all badly kept, crammed one on top of the other, and downright lousy too. Why, it made me itch all over when I had to clean and throw away half the stuff! All that's sold there, I mean, rugs that

are not even new, cracked pottery, everything second
hand, so to speak. And the children, Madame! Scores of
them, crawling on the bare ground, and half-naked too!
And what about the men! Handsome fellows, Madame,
who stroll along, never in a hurry—with a little bunch
of roses, or violets, in their hand, or even tucked behind
their ear, like a Spanish dancer! And nobody puts them
to shame."

" . . . ?"

"The country round about? I don't know. It's like
here. The land is cultivated. When the weather's good
it's quite pretty."

" . . . ?"

"What sort of plants? Exotic? Oh! yes, like in Monte
Carlo? Yes, yes there are palm trees. And also little
flowers, that I don't know the names of. And then, lots
of thistles. The people over there pick them and stick
them on to long thorns, pretending they smell like white
carnations. White carnations may be all right for you,
but for me, smells just give me a headache!"

" . . . ?"

"No. I've not seen nothing else. What do you take us
for? We have our work, and that comes first. My routine
in the morning, to start with, then a friction, then my
complete toilet, and by then it's breakfast-time. Coffee
and the daily papers, then I get busy with my work.
D'you think it's a joke to keep two people spotless,
underwear and all, without mentioning our stage-tights
and costumes? I couldn't stick a stain or a missing
stitch . . . that's how I am! Between Saint-Etienne and
Tunis I made myself six slips and six pairs of under-pants,
and I'd have completed the dozen, had Hector not
fancied he needed flannel waistcoats! And then there's the
dressing-room to be kept clean, the hotel room has to

be tidied up, expenses accounted for, money to be banked. I'm very particular, you see."

" . . . "

"Now you, who talk so much of travel, now you just take Bucharest! Never did a town bring me such trouble! The establishment had recently been renovated and the damp plaster-work sweated. At night, what with the heating and the lights, the walls of our dressing-room simply dripped water. I noticed that at once, and lucky I did, for imagine the mess it would have made of our stage costumes! You should have seen me every evening, at midnight, dragging about my two sequined dresses, the ones I wear in the whirl-wind waltz, one in each hand, on a couple of coat-hangers! And every day at nine I had to bring them back. Now please tell me if I could come away with happy memories of that town."

" . . . ?"

"Oh, you just leave me alone with your travel-mania! You won't make me change my mind on that subject, and I've visited enough countries, I can tell you. Towns, the world over, they're all the same! You'll always find first, a music-hall to work in; second, a tavern, Munich-styled, to eat in; third, a bad hotel to sleep in. When you've been all round the world, you'll think like me. Over and above that, there are nasty people everywhere, so one has to learn to keep one's distance; and one can count oneself lucky when one comes into contact, like today, with people who are good company and have class."

" . . . !"

"But not at all! No flattery intended, believe me. *Au revoir*, Madame, until tonight. When you've finished your number, I'll have the pleasure of introducing you to my husband, who will be as delighted as I was myself to make your acquaintance."

THE WORKROOM

A SMALL third-floor dressing-room, little more than a cramped closet with a single window opening on a narrow side-street. An over-heated radiator dries up the air, and every time the door opens the funnel of the spiral staircase belches up, like a chimney-stack, all the heat from the lower floors, saturated with the human odour of some sixty performers and the even more potent stench of a certain little place, situated near by.

Five girls are packed in here, with five rush-seated stools jammed between the make-up table and the recess in which are hung, hidden and protected by a greyish curtain, their costumes for the *Revue*. Here they live every night from seven-thirty till twenty minutes after midnight and, twice a week, for matinées, from half past one till six. Anita is the first to come in, rather out of breath, but with cool cheeks and moist lips. She shrinks back and exclaims: "Lord above! It's not possible to stay in here, it turns you up!"

She soon becomes accustomed to it, coughs a little, then doesn't give it another thought, since she only just has time to undress and make up. Her frock and under-slip are removed quicker than a pair of gloves and can be hung up anywhere. But there comes a moment when she curbs her haste and her face assumes a serious expression. Anita cautiously extracts two long pins from her hat, and carefully sticks them back through the same holes. Then, under the four turned-up corners of an outspread newspaper, she religiously protects that garish yet mingy edifice that contrives to look like a combination of a Red Indian headress, a Phrygian cap and a dressed salad. For everyone knows that grease-powder, flying in clouds from shaken puffs, spells death to velvet and feathers.

Wilson, the second on the scene, enters with a vacant look, hardly awake.

"Listen! Hell! I'd got something to tell you. . . . I must have swallowed it on the way."

She, too, takes off her hat according to established rites, then lifts a fringe of fair hair off her forehead, to disclose an incompletely healed scar.

"You can't imagine how my head still throbs from it!"

"Serves you right," interrupts Anita in a dry tone. "If you will go and get half the scenery on your 'nut', and if this happens in a joint where the managers are mean enough to send you home with tuppence-worth of ether on a handkerchief—without even paying the cab-fare or the doctor's fee—so that you have to stay put, half dead, for a whole week, and if you haven't even the self-respect to sue the management, then you do not complain, you just shut up. Now had it been me!"

Wilson does not reply, too busied—her features distorted by the effort—in trying to detach a long golden hair that is wickedly sticking to her wound. Besides, it is useless to answer back Anita, a born termagant and anarchist, always ready to "sue" or "get the story into the newspapers".

The three others arrive simultaneously: Régine Tallien, whose plump little housemaid's figure, abundantly furnished in front and behind, ironically casts her for page-boy parts, or "stylish male impersonations"; Maria Ancona, so dark she really believes herself a genuine Italian; and little Garcin, an obscure supernumerary, rather alarming, who flashes dark glances partly insincere, partly apprehensive, and is as thin as a starved cat.

They don't bother to pass the time of day, they meet

too often. No rivalry exists between them because, with the exception of Maria Ancona, who has a small solo in the tarentella, they all vegetate in chorus routine. Nor is it Maria Ancona's "part" that little Garcin envies her, but much more the brand new dyed fox fur round her neck. They are not friends either, yet from being thus thrown together, crowded and almost choked to death in their cribbed cabin, they have developed a sort of animal satisfaction, the cheerfulness of creatures in captivity. Maria Ancona sings as she unfastens her garters, held together by safety-pins, and her stays with broken laces. She laughs to find that her slip is torn under the arm and nettled by Régine Tallien, who wears the embroidered linen and stout cotton corsets of a well-behaved maidservant, she retorts: "Can't help it, my dear. I'm an artist by temperament! And d'you suppose I can keep my underwear clean with that horrible tin armour of mine!"

"Then do like me," whispers sly little Garcin; "don't wear any, any under-slips, I mean."

She is clothed only in a pair of trellised tights, all gold and pearls, with two openwork metal discs stuck over her non-existent breasts. The rough edges of her jewelled ornaments, the coarsely punched copper pendants, the clinking chain-armour she wears, scratch and mark her lean and apparently insensitive bare skin without her even noticing.

"Just admit," shouts Anita, "that the management ought to provide the slips worn on the stage! But you're all so thin-skinned, you're not even capable of claiming your dues!"

She turns a half made-up face towards her companions, a dead white mask with bright red goggles, that makes her look like a Polynesian warrior and, without even interrupting her tirade, she ties round her head a filthy silk rag, all that remains of a "wig-kerchief", intended to protect the hair from the brilliantine on the stage wigs.

"It's like this tattered duster I've got on my nut," continues Anita. "Yes, yes, go on saying it disgusts you, but I will-not-change-it! The management owes me one, and this *thing* can jolly well rot on my head, I will not replace it! My dues, that's all I care about."

Not one of them is carried away by her anarchic rage, knowing it to be merely verbal, and even little Wilson, wounded as she is, simply shrugs her shoulders.

The hour flies by, the unbreathable dryness of the air is now permeated by a hot dormitory smell. From time to time a dresser squeezes sideways into the room, somehow managing to move about, fastening a hook, tying the strings of stage-tights or the ribbons of a Greek buskin. Régine Tallien and Wilson have already fled, halberd in hand, to their medieval parade. Anita hastens behind Maria Ancona, because a voice from the staircase is calling out: "Ladies of the Tarantella, have I to come in person to fetch you?"

Little Garcin, whose asexual graces are kept in store for a "Byzantine Festival", now remains alone. Out of her sordid handbag she extracts a thimble, a pair of scissors, a piece of needlework already begun, and, perched on her rush-seated stool, she begins to sew with avid concentration.

"Oh!" cries Maria Ancona, returning hot and out of breath. "So she's already settled down to it!"

"What d'you expect," jealously echoes Anita, "for all the work she has to do on the stage!"

The sound of a cavalcade on the stairs and a shrill distant bell announce the end of the first act, bringing back Wilson, still slightly dazed and with an aching forehead, and Régine Tallien with her red man-at-arms wig. The daily break for the intermission, instead of bringing relaxation, seems to excite the girls. Off fly bicoloured tights and Neapolitan skirts, to be replaced by spongey dressing-gowns or cotton kimonos, mottled with the stains of cosmetics. Bare feet, unexpectedly bashful, grope under the make-up table for shapeless old slippers, while hands, pale or red, suddenly become cautious in unrolling lengths of linen and bits of imitation lace. They all inquisitively bend over Maria Ancona's unfinished "combination", the cynical little garment of a poor prostitute, outrageously transparent, sewn with broad, clumsy stitches. Little Garcin smocks fine muslin with the patience of a persistent mouse. Régine fills in her time hemming white handkerchiefs.

The five of them, now seated on their high rush stools, are busy and quiet, as if they had at last reached their goal at the end of the day. This half hour is theirs. And during this half hour they allow themselves, as a respite, the candid illusion of being cloistered young women who sew.

They suddenly fall silent, pacified by some unknown spell, and even the rowdy Anita gives no thought to her 'dues', and smiles mysteriously at a table-cloth embroidered in scarlet. In spite of their gaping wraps, of their high-pitched knees, of the insolent rouge still blossoming on their cheeks, they have the chaste attitude and bent backs of sedate seamstresses. And it is from the lips of little Garcin, naked in her beaded-net pants, that a childish little song, keeping time with her busy needle, involuntarily finds its way.

MATINÉE

"You see all those people in the char-à-bancs, don't you?—and those others in four-wheelers?—and again those in taxis? And you see the ones over there, in shirt-sleeves on their doorsteps, and those sitting outside the cafés? Very well then! All that crowd do not have to play in a matinée. D'you hear me?"

" . . . give a damn."

"But *you* are playing in a matinée!"

"Don't go on so, Brague!"

"I am playing in a matinée, too. We are playing in matinée. On Thursdays, and on Sundays too, we have a matinée."

I could slap him—were it not for the effort of lifting my arm. He continues, relentlessly. "There are also those who are not here, those who decamped to the country yesterday evening and won't come back to town till Monday. They're out under the trees, or taking a dip in the Marne. Well, they're doing what they're doing, but . . . *they are not appearing in a matinée!*

As our taxi jerks to an abrupt stop, the dry wind, which had been baking our faces, suddenly drops. I feel the pavement burning through the thin soles of my shoes. My cruel companion stops talking and purses his mouth, as much as to say: "Now it's becoming serious."

At the dark and narrow stage-door there is still a trace of musty coolness. The doorman, dozing in his chair, wakes up as we pass to brandish a newspaper.

"Ninety-six in the shade, eh!"

He throws this figure at us, in triumph, yet scared, as if it were the death-roll in some grand-scale catastrophe.

But we pass in silence, sparing of speech and movement, in fact jealous of this old man who keeps watch in a shady paradise, a paradise invaded by stale cellar smells and ammonia, on the threshold of our own inferno. Anyhow, what do ninety-six degrees mean? Ninety-six, or ninety-six thousand, it's all the same. We have no thermometer up there on our second floor. Ninety-six degrees on the tower of Saint-Jacques? And what will it rise to during this afternoon's matinée? How high will it be in my dressing-room, with its two windows, two right royal windows facing due south and shutterless?

"There's no saying," sighs Brague, as he enters his cubicle, "we must jolly well be 'above normal' up here!"

After a dismal glance, devoid even of entreaty, at the panes set ablaze by the sun, I let my clothes drop off without any relief: my skin can no longer look forward to the biting little draught between door and window that only a month ago nipped my bare shoulders.

A strange silence reigns within our crowded cells. Opposite mine, a half-open door allows me a glimpse of the backs of two seated men, in dirty bath-wraps, bending over their make-up table without a word passing. The electric bulb burns above their heads, anaemically pink in the radiant light of three o'clock in the afternoon.

A shrill note, a prolonged piercing cry, rises up to us from the depths of the theatre. This means that there really is at this very moment down there on the stage a rigidly corsetted woman, swathed in the long, tight-fitting dress so dear to lady novelists, who has achieved the miracle of smiling, singing, and reaching the gods with her high-pitched C, that makes my parched tongue thirst for slices of lemon, for unripe gooseberries, for all things acid, fresh and green.

What a sigh answers mine from a near-by dressing-room, such a tragic sigh, almost a sob! Surely it must come from that chit of a girl barely recovered from a bout of bronchial-fever, the fragile little ballad-singer, exhausted by this savage heat, who peps herself up by drinking iced absinthes.

My cold-cream is unrecognisable, reduced to cloudy oil that smells of petrol. A melted paste, the colour of rancid butter, is all that remains of my white grease-foundation. The liquefied contents of my rouge-jar might well be used "to colour", as cooks say, a dish of "*Pêches Cardinal*".

For better or worse, here I am at last anointed with these multicoloured fats, and heavily powdered. I still have time, before our mimodrama, to survey a face on which glow, in the sunshine, the mixed hues of purple petunia, begonia and the afternoon blue of a morning glory. But the energy to move, walk, dance and mime, where can I hope to find that?

The sun has sunk a little, releasing one of my windows which I hasten to fling open; but the sill burns my hands, and the narrow mews below reeks of rotting melons and unwatered gutters. Two hatless women have pitched their chairs in the middle of the street and stare up at the powdery sky, like animals about to be drowned.

A hesitant step slowly mounts the stairs. I turn round at the moment when a frail little dancer dressed as a Red Indian reaches our landing: she is quite pale despite her make-up, and her temples are black with sweat. We look at each other without uttering a word. Then she lifts towards me the hem of her emboidered costume, weighted down with glass beads, strips of leather, metal and pearls, and murmurs as she goes back to her dressing-room, "And with all these trappings it must weigh eighteen pounds!"

The call-bell is the only sound to break the silence. On my way down I pass stage-hands, half-stripped and mute. Girls of the Andalusian ballet cross the foyer in full costume, without any greeting other than a ferocious glance at the great mirror. Brague, suffering agonies under the black cloth of his short waistcoat and skin-tight Spanish trousers, whistles out of sheer vanity to show that he's "not going to snuff out like the others!" An enormously fat boy, round as a barrel in his inn-keeper's clothes, looks about to suffocate and terrifies me: supposing he were to die on the stage!

Somehow or other, the mysterious forces of discipline and musical rhythm, together with an arrogant and childish desire to appear handsome, to appear strong, all combine to lead us on. To be truthful, we perform exactly as we always do! The prostrated public, invisible in the darkened auditorium, notices nothing that it should not, the short breaths that parch our lungs, the perspiration that soaks us and stains our silk costumes, the moustache of sweat and drying powder that so tactlessly gives me a virile upper lip. Nor must it notice the exhausted expression on its favourite comic's face, the wild glint in his eyes as though he were ready to bite. Above all none must guess at the nervous repulsion that makes me shrink back at touching and feeling only damp hands, arms, cheeks or necks! Damp sleeves, glued hair, sticky tumblers, handkerchiefs like sponges—everything is moist or ringing wet, myself included.

Once the curtain has fallen we separate hastily, somehow ashamed of being the wretched, steaming flock we are. We hurry on down to the street, yearning for the dry dusty evening, towards the illusion of coolness shed by the already high-riding moon, fully visible, yet warm and lustreless.

THE STARVELING

In the first act of the play in which we are touring he takes the part of a profligate; whereas, in the third, he is transformed by a red wig and a neat white apron into a waiter.

When the time comes to catch our train, at dawn or late at night—for this is a strenuous tour, playing thirty-three towns in thirty-three days—he never fails to arrive late and in a rush, so that all I knew of him was a slim figure with his overcoat flying, agitated beyond measure by his race against time. The manager and my companions would wave their arms and shout at him.

"Come on, Gonzalez, for God's sake! One of these days you'll miss it for good!"

He would float into the gaping second-class carriage as on the wings of a whirlwind, so that I never had time to see his face.

Then, the other day, on the station at Nîmes, when I suddenly exclaimed "There's a scent of hyacinths! Who smells of hyacinths?", with a polite, restrained little gesture he turned to offer me the nosegay that adorned his buttonhole.

Since that day I have taken more notice of him and, like the others, I raise my arms in despair when he arrives late, shouting in chorus: "Come on Gonzalez, for God's sake!" and I even recognise his face.

A sallow little face, so biliously pale that one imagines his 'foundation-make-up' has penetrated his skin. A face all bumps and hollows, cheek-bones protruding above deep-sunk cheeks, the eyebrows too thick, the mouth thin above an obstinate chin.

But why, I wonder, does he never remove his overcoat that is faded near the shoulders from last year's sun and rain? A glance at his shoes provides the answer. Gonzalez exposes to the daylight, and my inspection, unspeakably shoddy footwear, the cracks and crevices of their once gleaming patent-leather only aggravated by the cheap polish of third-rate inns. His shoes lead my thoughts to his trousers, ever mysterious under the ample folds of his overcoat, and to his shirt-collar, mercifully all but hidden behind an amazing black cravat wound thrice round his neck.

His clumsily mended cotton gloves refute any illusion I may have that this little comedian affects the "showing-off-indifference" of a young bohemian, for they spell destitution. Once again I am confronted with genuine poverty. When, if ever, shall I cease to find it? Now I pay real attention to this boy, wait for his breathless arrival, notice that he does not smoke, carries no umbrella, that his suitcase is falling to pieces and that he discreetly watches for the moment when he can pick up the daily paper after I have read it through and dropped it.

Warned by some bashful instinct, he in his turn now takes notice of me. He openly smiles at me, and presses in his warm skinny hand the fingers I extend towards him; yet he is careful, a moment later, to vanish and make himself as scarce as possible. He never joins us when we lunch in station buffets, and I cannot remember having seen Gonzalez at the same table as the less moneyed of our good companions for the "light meal at one franc fifty". Once he performed his disappearing act at Tarascon, whilst we were devouring an omelet cooked in oil, tepid veal and colourless chicken. He came back when the acorn-flavoured coffee was being served; he came back spare, gay, carefree—"I've been to have a look at the neighbourhood"—a pink carnation in his mouth and croissant-crumbs in the folds of his clothes.

I confess I'm worried about this boy; I don't dare to make further enquiries. I set childish traps for him.

"Will you have some coffee, Gonzalez?"

"Thanks, but it's forbidden me. Nerves . . . you know."

"That's not nice of you! The round's on me today. You surely won't be the only one to refuse?"

"Oh, well, if you make it a question of comradeship. . . ."

Another day, at Lourdes, I bought two dozen little hot sausages.

"Come on, children, don't let them get cold! Buck up Gonzalez, or you'll miss the lot! Snatch those two quickly, before Hautefeuille pounces on them: he's quite fat enough as it is."

I watched him eat, with the sneaking curiosity of one expecting that some movement on his part, a famished sigh, might betray his ill-satisfied hunger. Finally I decided to put a casual question to our manager.

"How much is Martineau getting nowadays? And that thinggummy over there, young Gonzalez?"

"Martineau is paid fifteen francs, because he plays in the curtain-raiser as well as the main piece. Gonzalez gets only twelve francs a night—we're not on a Grand Duke's tour!"

Twelve francs. . . . Let's see how I reckon his expenses! He sleeps in joints at one fifty to two francs per night. Ten per cent for valeting, a problematical *café-au-lait*, but count two meals at two fifty for the price of one. Let's add another franc and a half for trams and buses . . . plus the gentlemen's flowered buttonholes! Well then, this young man can live within it, he can exist quite comfortably. I felt relieved and in the evening, during the interval, I shook his hand as if he'd just inherited a fortune! Taking courage from the semi-darkness and the fact that our faces were disguised by make-up, he allowed an anxious cry to escape his lips.

"It's drawing to a close, eh! Only thirteen more days! Oh for a tour that would last a whole life-time! How I dream of it!"

"You like your work as much as that?"

He shrugged his shoulders: "My work, my work! Naturally, I rather like it, but it's given me plenty of worries for my run. . . . Besides, thirty-three days, it's short. . . ."

"What d'you mean, short?"

"Short for what I want to do! Now, listen. . . ."

He suddenly sat down beside me, on a dusty garden-bench used for the last act, began to talk, began feverishly to tell me the story of his life.

"Now listen. . . . I can really talk to you, can't I? You've been kind . . . a real good companion to me. I have to take back two hundred francs."

"Take back where?"

"To Paris . . . if I want to eat during the coming month, and the one after. I can't face going through all that I've endured a second time, my health won't stand it."

"You've been ill?"

"Ill, if you like. Being broke is a damned illness."

With a professional gesture he ran his forefingers along his false moustache, which is in the habit of getting unstuck, and averted his blue-rimmed sunken eyes.

"There's no shame in admitting it. I played the fool, left my father, who is a book-binder, to get into the theatre. That was two years ago. My father cursed me, then . . ."

"What d'you mean? Your father has . . ."

" . . . Cursed me." Gonzalez repeated, with theatrical simplicity. "Cursed me, gave me a proper cursing. I found work with the Grenelle-les-Gobelins company. That's when I started not eating enough. When summer came, I hadn't a sou in my pocket. For six months I lived on the twenty-five francs a month an aunt of mine let me have . . . secretly."

"Good Lord! Twenty-five francs! How did you manage?"

He laughed, in a rather mad way, gazing straight in front of him.

"I don't know. It's plain murder, I don't know now how I got along. I no longer remember very clearly. My mind went blank. I remember I had a suit, one shirt, one collar, no change of anything. . . . The rest I've forgotten."

He was silent for a moment while he extended both legs with care, to ease his already threadbare trousers over his kneejoints.

"Then after that I had a few weeks in the *Fantaisies Parisiennes,* at the Comédie Mondaine. But the going was bad. You need a stomach for that and I no longer have one. The pay's so miserably small. I've got no name, no clothes, no craft outside the theatre, no savings. I can't see myself making old bones!"

He laughed again, just as the spot-light came on, throwing into sharp relief his fleshless head, his hard cheek-bones, the dark sockets of his eyes, and the too wide slit of his mouth, for the lips were swallowed up by the contraction of his laughter.

"So, you see then, I have to take back two hundred and twenty francs. With that sum I'm safe for two months, at least. This tour was like winning a prize in a lottery, I can tell you. . . . Have I bored you stiff with my stories?"

I had no time to answer him: the stage-bell started to ring above our heads, and Gonzalez, incurably late, fluttered off to his dressing-room with all the lightness of a dead leaf, with the airy macabre grace of a young skeleton, dancing.

LOVE

BECAUSE she is fair-haired and young, a rather skinny girl with huge blue eyes, she fulfils exactly all the requirements we expect of a "little English dancer". She speaks some French, with all the vigour of a young duckling, and to articulate these few words of our language she expends a useless energy which brings a flush to her cheeks and makes her eyes sparkle.

When she emerges from the dressing-room she shares with her companions next to mine, and walks down towards the stage, ready made-up and in costume, I can't distinguish her from the other girls, for she strives, as is most fitting, to be just an impersonal and attractive little English dancer in a Revue! When the first girl comes out, followed by the second, and the third, then the others up to the ninth, they all greet me, as they pass, with the same happy smile, a similar nod of the head that sets their pinkish-blonde false curls bobbing in the same way. The nine faces are painted with identical make-up, cleverly tinted with mauve around the eyes, while the lids are burdened, on each of their lashes, with such a heavy touch of mascara, that it is impossible to distinguish the true colour of the pupil.

But when they leave, at ten past midnight, having hastily wiped their cheeks with the corner of a towel and

re-powdered them chalky white, their eyes still barbar-
ously enlarged, or when they come to rehearse in the
afternoon, punctually at one o'clock, I immediately
recognise little Gloria, a genuine blonde, with two puffs
of frizzy hair tied round the temples with a strip of black
velvet inside her hideous hat like a bird nesting in an old
basket. Her upper lip protrudes a little from two pointed
canines, and this makes her look, in repose, as if she
were sucking a white sugared almond.

I don't know why I noticed her. She is not as pretty
as Daisy, that dark-haired demon, always in tears or in a
rage, who dances with devilish gusto and then escapes
to the top of the staircase, whence she spits out objection-
able English expletives. She is less attractive than the
awful Edith, who exaggerates her accent to raise a laugh
and, with assumed candour, utters French indecencies,
well aware of their meaning.

Yet Gloria, who is dancing for the first time in France,
compels my attention. She is sweet and touching, in an
anonymous way. She has never called the ballet-master
'damned fool', and her name never appears on the board
where the list of fines are posted. Admittedly, she
shrieks when she runs up or down the two flights of
steps leading to the stage; but she shrieks like the others,
instinctively, and because a bunch of English girls, who
change their costumes four times between nine o'clock
and midnight, cannot run up and down staircases without
yelling like Red Indians or singing inordinately loud.
Gloria, therefore, lets her comically youthful falsetto
mingle with the inevitable hubbub and she equally well
holds her own in the girls' common dressing-room,
separated from mine by a rickety wooden partition.

These travelling show-girls have turned their rectangular

closet into a real gipsy encampment. Red and black
cosmetic pencils roll all over their make-up table, covered
at one end with brown paper and at the other with a
tattered old towel. The slightest draught would blow
away the postcards fastened to the walls with pins stuck
in at a slant. The jar of rouge, the Leichner eyebrow
pencil, the woollen powder puff, could all be carried
away in a knotted kerchief, and these little girls, off and
away in a couple of months, will leave fewer traces of
their passage here than would a troop of wandering
Romanies, whose halting place is marked by round
patches of singed grass and the flaky ashes of fires
kindled with stolen wood.

" . . . 'k you," says Gloria in an educated voice.
"The pleasure is mine," our good companion Marcel
politely replies. Though billed as a tenor, he may well
be dancing this coming month or even performing in a
drama at the Gobelins or in a Revue at Montrouge.

As if by mere chance, Marcel waits on the landing for
the return of the noisy flock of English show girls. By
apparent chance, too, Gloria comes up last and lingers
for a moment, time enough to fumble with awkward
grace in the paper-bag of lemon-drops our good companion offers her.

I take careful note of the slow progress of this idyll. He
is young, famished, ardent, firmly determined not to
"break down", and looks—in spite of his well-worn tails
and artificial lily-of-the-valley buttonhole—like a handsome, crafty working-class boy. But Gloria's strange
foreign manners baffle him. With a French chum, a little
Paris music-hall sparrow, he would already know where
he stood—things work, or they don't—but he simply
can't fathom this funny *anglishe*. She may rush off the

stage, dishevelled and yelling, hastily unhooking her dress, yet when she reaches the landing she pulls herself together, straightens her face to accept and acknowledge the proffered sweet with the dignified " . . . 'k you" of a young lady in full evening dress.

She attracts him. She irritates him too. Sometimes he shrugs his shoulders as he watches her walk away, but I can feel that it is at himself he is poking fun. The other day he chucked into Gloria's large hat, held dangling by its ribbons, half a dozen tangerines, seized on at once by the horde of blonde savages, who snatched at them with triumphant shrieks, loud laughter and sharp nails.

This long flirtation exasperates the impatient French boy, lively and inconstant, whereas Gloria revels in its protraction. She now calls Marcel by his name: *Mâss'l*, and has given him a picture postcard of herself. Not the one in which she is dressed as a toddler with a hoop, nor that on which she is disguised as a "Poulbot kid," with a hole in her pants—oh no!—but the loveliest of all, presenting Gloria as a Medieval Lady wearing a high headdress, a quasi-regal Gloria.

They don't seem worried at being unable to talk to each other. With subtle shrewdness the boy sets out to be assidious and unassuming. Have I not seen him kiss a thin little hand, one that was not withdrawn, a bony little paw, chapped by cold water and liquid white! But, on the sly, he looks at Gloria with indiscreet persistence, as if he were choosing in advance the proper place to implant a kiss. Once behind the closed door of the dressing-room, she sings for him, then shouts his name "*Mâss'l*", as if she were throwing him flowers.

In short, things go well: even too well. . . . This quasi-mute idyll unfurls like a mimodrama, with no other music than Gloria's exuberant voice and no words but the name *Mâss'l*, diversified by love's numberless inflexions. After the first radiant *Mâss'ls*, shouted on a slightly nasal note, I have heard lower *Mâss'ls*, provocative and tender, exacting too—and then, one fine day, came a tremulous *Mâss'l*, so low that it sounded like an entreaty.

Tonight, I fear, I am hearing it for the last time. At the head of the staircase, hovering on its top step, I find a forlorn little Gloria, with a distorted wig, crying humbly, all over her make-up, and repeating under her breath "Mâss'l" . . . "*Mâss'l* . . ."

THE HARD WORKER

"YOUR arms, Hélène! Your arm control! That's the second time your hand has struck your head while you're dancing! I've told you again and again, my girl: the arms must curve like handles above your head, as if you were balancing a basket of flowers!"

Hélène answers with a sullen out-of-patience look only, and corrects the position of her arms. She's ready to launch forth again on the studio floor—a well-worn shiny parquet-floor, battered by the raps of heels and the ballet-master's wand—when she changes her mind, and cries out: "Are you still there, Robert?"

"Of course," replies a submissive voice from the other side of the door.

"Supposing you took the car and popped over to the furrier's and told him I won't be coming till tomorrow?"

No answer; but I hear the tap, tap of a walking stick and the sound of the front door being closed: "Robert" has gone.

"So much the better!" murmurs Hélène in a softened oice. "It exasperates me to feel he's there waiting for me and doing nothing."

Twice a week I sit through the last minutes of Hélène Gromet's dancing lesson: she is put through her paces from four to five, just before my own turn comes. She treats me more as a colleague than a friendly companion, much as if we were workers in the same factory; by which I mean that we talk little but seriously, and that sometimes she reveals her feelings with the same cool candour as when confiding in her masseuse or her pedicure.

Hélène is not a real dancer, but a "little piece who dances". She made her music-hall *début* last season, in Revue, and, as her first attempt, she "flung" at her audience two scabrous little ditties, putting them across at the top of her brand new, unsophisticated, brassy voice, without any of the simperings of false modesty, but with a perfectly straight face, and with an aggressive innocence that enchanted. Substantial offers of work, a no less substantial "friend", two motor-cars, a string of pearls and a mink coat, were all showered on Hélène in one single stroke of luck—but her steady little head never wavered. She boasts of being a "hard worker", and sticks to her ungainly, plebeian name.

"Do you imagine I'm going to re-christen myself? A simple name, not too pretty, that's what puts you straight into the top class. Look at Badet and Bordin!"

All her entries amount to a miniature apotheosis. The subdued thunder of a motor-car heralds her approach, then she appears, weighed down under ermine and velvet, a trembling cloud of osprey feathers in her hat. A decisive and carefully devised make-up standardises her youthful face under a mask of dead white powder, with pink touches on the cheeks and chin. Her blued eyelids carry a heavy double fringe of lashes, stiff with mascara, and her teeth shine almost woundingly against the purplish lipstick that outlines her mouth.

"I know I'm young enough to do without all that muck," Hélène explains, "but it's now part of my array, and it's useful too. For like this I am made up for life. I'll have nothing to add when I'm twenty years older. Under this coating I can afford to look ill or to have tired eyes; it's as practical as a disguise. For you'd better know, I do nothing without good reason."

This young utilitarian scares me. She takes her lesson as she would swallow a glass of cod-liver oil: conscientiously, and to the bitter end. Nevertheless it is a pleasure to watch her exercise, flexible and well balanced on her clever legs. She is pretty, and touchingly young. What then does she lack? For she does lack something.

"Your smile, Hélène, your smile!" exclaims the ballet-mistress. "Don't put on your cashier's face. You don't seem to realise that you're dancing, my child."

The former ballerina's broad and blotched face endeavours in vain to teach Hélène that the lips must part to disclose the teeth, while the corners of the mouth must curve upwards like the horns of a crescent moon. And I can't help laughing at the commercial composure of the pupil, as she faces her grinning teacher with a thoughtful brow and a rigid, painted mouth.

What are the thoughts of this obstinate child, this insensitive bee? She often repeats: "When one wants to get *somewhere* . . ." Get somewhere, but where? What suspended mirage keep her eyes uplifted when she seems to look through me, through the walls, through the submissive features of her admiring young "friend"?

She is tense, and appears to aim relentlessly at some

concealed goal. Glory? no . . . those who seek glory admit it, and I have never heard Hélène Gromet express a desire for glamorous parts or proudly say "When I can rival Simone . . ." Money! That sounds more likely. At the finish of a lively lesson, like today's, it is from her fatigue that I best discover in Hélène the solid little "child of the people", eager to earn and to hoard.

She bears her fatigue with the air of graceful fulfilment, the happily satisfied expression of a young washerwoman who has just put down her load of freshly laundered linen. Scantily clothed in a damp under-slip and a tiny pair of silk knickers, she comes to sit beside me on the side-bench. She has crossed her legs and remains silent, one shoulder hunched, while her bare arms hang limp.

As the twilight deepens, the black undulations of her hair seems tinged with a deeper blue.

My imagination conjures up somewhere, in some poor place, Hélène's mama who, returning at this same hour from the trough by the river, lets her reddened arms hang loose in just the same way: or a sister, or a brother, who has just left a workshop or a stuffy office. They too are punctual, and bent, and temporarily weary, like Hélène.

She rests a while before re-doing her face, with the aid of a fat powder puff and a small pad of rouged cotton-wool. With the trusting calm of a drowsy animal she allows me to see on her dark-skinned undressed face the tawniness and slightly coarse grain that most common mortals ignore. In a moment or two a surfeit of powder will blur the sharply arched curve of her imperious nose, not unlike that of a bird of prey.

The return of "Robert" brings her to her feet, and immediately puts her on the defensive. Yet he is only a fair-haired rather humble boy, eager to wait on her and help her to dress, fastening the shiny straps of her little shoes and pulling the long pink lace of her stays. The pair of them together barely miss making an enchanting picture.

I can see she does not hate him, but I cannot see that she loves him either. The attention she grants him shows no subservience. When they leave together, she takes full stock of him with that penetrating, antagonistic look of hers, as if he were yet another lesson to be learned. And I feel, at times, very much like seizing this avaricious child's arm and asking her: "But, Hélène, what about Love?"

AFTER MIDNIGHT

"How nice it is here."

The little dancer rubs her bare arms, the rather red, coarse-skinned arms of an undernourished blonde, and breathes in the hot dry air of the restaurant as if it were ozone.

On a polished strip of linoleum in the centre of the big dining-room a few couples are already revolving, among them a girl from Normandy in the lace head-dress of the Caux district, a painted hussy with a red silk scarf, an Egyptian dancing girl, and a curly-headed baby wearing a tartan sash. This establishment, highly rated on the Riviera, employs some dozen dance hostesses and as many singers.

Little Maud comes on here from the Eldorado, where she croons and gambols through an "English Number". She has just arrived, after running all the way through an icy wind, to earn her twenty francs pittance at the "Restaurant of the Good Hostess", from midnight till six in the morning.

She flexes her knee joints a little as she leans against the wall, and, after a rough calculation of her dancing at both performances at the Eldorado, and now waltzing here till dawn, finds it amounts to seven hours of valse and cake-walk, not counting dressing and undressing, rubbing on and removing her make-up. She was hungry enough when she arrived, but her appetite has been stayed by a glass of beer gulped down in the artistes' room. 'So much the better,' she reflects, 'I've not got to get fat.'

Maud's attraction lies in her angular girlish slimness; she is labelled English because of her fair hair, reddish elbows, and her funny little tippler's nose, blotchy round the nostrils. She has acquired a vicious little smile, and learned to shake her schoolgirl locks and hide her face behind her square-fingered paws, chapped by liquid white, at any suggestion of a risky joke. In private life she is simply a "Caf'-Con'" girl like any of the others, overworked, innocent of malice or coquetry, for ever on the move from hotel to train, from station to theatre, ever tormented by hunger, lack of sleep, and the morrow's insecurity.

For the time being she takes a rest on her feet, like a saleswoman in a big store, and keeps worrying a recent hole in her flesh-tinted tights with her big toe. 'Five francs for invisible mending!'

One hand absentmindedly smoothes the creases in the hem of her babyish satin frock, once Nile green, now yellow. 'Dry-cleaning, ten francs. Hell, that eats up my night's earnings! If only that tipsy little lady would come back, the one who was here the night of the masked ball, and threw me the change from her bill!'

A violinist in an embroidered Roumanian shirt plays *You once vowed to be mine* with such amorous intensity that he is smothered in encores.

'So much the better,' she says to herself once more. 'How I wish he'd play all night long, for then I'd be living on unearned income!'

Her fond hopes are dashed. A wink from the manager orders her to waltz, clinging to the shoulders of a sham toreador, thin and willowy and far too tall for her. Maud is so tired by this time that she waltzes without being aware of it, hanging on to the youth who clasps her to him with professional, almost indecent unconcern. Everything swirls about her. The head of a hat-pin, the clasp of a necklace, the setting of a ring, pierce her eyes as she dances round. The polished floor glides under her feet, glistening, soapy, as if wet.

'If I go on waltzing for very long tonight,' she muses in a daze, 'I'll end up without a thought in my head.'

She shuts her eyes and abandons herself to her partner's insensitive breast, throwing herself into the whirl with the trustful semi-consciousness of a child ready to drown. But the music stops suddenly, and the toreador lets his charge drop without a glance, without a word, like flotsam, on the nearest table.

Maud smiles, passes a hand across her forehead, and looks around. 'Ah, there's my "sympathetic couple".' For, every night, she picks out among those supping at The Good Hostess a couple who catch her fancy—in all innocence—and on whom she lavishes her most childish smiles, occasionally blowing them a kiss, or throwing them a flower; a couple whose departure brings her a short pang of regret, when she watches the woman rise to go with the air of regal boredom befitting one who knows she is being followed by an enamoured escort.

'How sweet they are this evening, my sympathetic couple!'

Sweet . . . in a way. Maud chooses to see things in that

way. A restless, vindictive desire seems to possess the man, who is very young and can barely conceal his impatience. His eyes are bright and shifty, and so constantly changing in colour that they turn pale more often than his tanned face. He eats hurriedly, as if he had a train to catch. When his glance catches his companion's, he throws his head back as if a bunch of too fragrant flowers had touched his nostrils.

She had arrived looking happy and self-assured, stimulated by the cold outside and a hearty appetite. She had clasped her hands under her chin and then asked the violinist in the embroidered shirt to play waltzes, more waltzes, and still more waltzes. He played for her *You once vowed to be mine. . . . Now you will never know! . . . Your heart was cruel.*

"Oh, how I adore that music!" she had sighed aloud.

She had smiled at Maud as she whirled past. And then she had fallen silent, gazing intently at her companion. "Leave me alone," she told him, pulling away the hand he was stroking.

'They're sweet, but they seem to quarrel without a word passing, 'Maud observes. 'They may be in love, but they're not true friends.'

Now the woman is leaning back in her chair, never taking her eyes off the ferocious eater facing her. Maud is fascinated by the woman's slender, feverish face, as though something were soon about to happen. The manager clacks his tongue to no purpose, in his attempt to recall the little dancer to her duty; Maud lingers on, bound by some mysterious telepathy to the woman who sits there, speechless, separated from her friend by gulfs of music, drifting further from him, perhaps, at every throbbing note of the violin, with despairing clairvoyance.

'They love each other, but they're ill at ease in each

other's company.' Such devotion wells up in the woman's dark glances, yet she remains obstinately silent as though fearful of bursting into tears or unburdening her heart in a flood of banal complaints. Her eyes are beautiful, eloquent and frightened, and seem to be telling the man: "You're a clumsy lover. . . . You don't begin to understand me. . . . I don't really know you, and you scare me. . . . You sneer at everything I like. . . . You lie so well! . . . You possess me completely, yet I can't trust you. . . . If you knew what limpid springs you wall up within me because I fear you! What am I doing here at your side? Would that this music could free me of you for ever! Or else that this violin would stop before I find out any more about you! You yearn for my undoing, not my happiness, and what is worst in me assures you of your victory."

Maud sighs 'Oh, what an ill assorted pair they are this evening! She ought to leave him, but . . .'

"Come along," the man murmurs as he stands up.

His companion rises to her feet, tall, black and glittering, like an obedient serpent, under the threat of his two bright eyes, so caressing, so treacherous. Defenceless, she follows him, with no support other than the sisterly smile of a little blonde dancer, who inwardly regrets the exit of her "sympathetic couple" and whose pout seems to indicate a reproachful 'Already?'

"LOLA"

FROM my dressing-room I could hear, every night, the tap-tap of heavy crutches on the iron steps leading up to the stage.

Yet there was no "Cripple's Number" on our programme. I used to open my door to watch the midget pony climbing the stairs on its nimble unshod feet. The white donkey followed clip-clopping behind, then the piebald Great Dane on its thick soft paws, then the beige poodle and the fox terriers.

Bringing up the rear, the plump Viennese lady in charge of the "Miniature Circus" would herself supervise the ascent of the tiny brown bear, always reluctant and somehow desperate, clutching at the bannisters and moaning as he mounted, like a punished child being sent up to bed. Two monkeys followed, in flounced silk sprinkled with sequins, smelling like an ill-kept chicken run. All of them climbed with stifled sighs, subdued groans and inaudible expletives; they were on their way up to await their daily hour's work.

I never again wished to see them up there, under full control and tame; the sight of their submissiveness had become intolerable to me. I knew too well that the martingaled pony tried in vain to toss its head and constantly pawed with one of its front legs, in a sort of ataxic jerk. I knew that the ailing, melancholic monkey would close its eyes and let its head rest in childish despair on its companion's shoulder; that the stupid Great Dane would stare into vacancy, gloomy and rigid, while the old poodle would wag its tail with senile benevolence; above all I knew that the pathetic little brown bear would seize its head in both paws, whimpering and almost in tears, because a very narrow strap fastened round its muzzle cut into its lip.

I should have liked to forget the entire misery-stricken group, in their white leather harness hung with jingle-bells and adorned with ribbons and bows, forget their slavering jaws, the rasping breath of these starved animals; I never again wanted to witness, and pity, this dumb animal distress I could do nothing to alleviate. So I remained down below, with Lola.

Lola did not come to visit me straight away. She waited until the sounds of the laborious ascent had died away, till the last fox-terrier had whisked its rump, white as a rabbit's scut, round the angle of the stairs. Only then did she push my half-open door with her long insinuating nose.

She was so white that her presence lit up my sordid dressing-room. A slim, elongated greyhound body, white as snow; her neck, her leg joints, her flanks and tail, bristled with fine silver; her fleecy coat shone like spun glass. She walked in and looked up at me with eyes of orange melting into brown, a colour so rare that it alone was enough to touch my heart. Her tongue hung out a little, pink and dry, and she panted gently from thirst. . . . "Give me a drink. Give me a drink, though I know it's forbidden. My companions up there are thirsty too, none of us are allowed to drink before working time. But you'll give me a drink."

She lapped up the luke-warm water I poured into an enamelled basin I had first rinsed out for her. She lapped it with an elegance that appeared, as did all her movements, to be an affectation and, in front of her, I felt ashamed of the chipped rim of the basin, of the dented jug, of the greasy walls she took good care to avoid.

While she drank I looked at her little winglike ears, at her legs, slender and firm as a hind's; at her fleshless ribs and beautiful nails, white as her coat.

Her thirst quenched, she turned away her coy tapering muzzle from the basin, and for a little while longer gazed at me with a look in which I could read nothing but vague anxiety, a sort of wild animal prayer. After that she went up by herself to the stage, where her performance was limited, it must be added, to an honorary appearance, to jumping a few obstacles which she took with accomplished grace, with a lazy, concealed strength. The footlights heightened the gold in her eyes, and she answered each crack of the whip with a nervous grimace, a menacing smile which disclosed the pink of her gums and her faultless teeth.

For nearly a month she begged no more of me than luke-warm, insipid water from a chipped basin. Every evening I used to say to her, but not in words, "Take it, though I am pining to give you all that is your due. For you have recognised me and deemed me worthy of quenching your thirst, you, who speak to no one, not even to the Viennese lady whose podgy, masterful hands fasten a blue collar round your serpent neck."

On the twenty-ninth day, sorrowfully, I kissed her flat silky forehead, and on the thirtieth . . . I bought her.

"Beautiful, but not a brain in her head," the Viennese lady confided to me. By way of a farewell, she chirped a few Austro-Hungarian endearments into Lola's ear, while the bitch stood beside me, serious, gazing straight in front of her, a hard look on her face, and squinting slightly. Whereupon I picked up her dangling leash and walked away, and the long brittle spindles, armed with ivory claws, fell into step behind me.

She escorted rather than followed me, and I held her chain high, so as not to inflict its weight on my captive princess. Would the ransom I had paid for her make her really mine?

Lola did not eat that day, and refused to drink the fresh water I offered her in a white bowl bought specially for her. But she languidly turned her undulating neck, her delicate feverish nose, toward the old chipped basin.

Out of this she consented to drink, and then looked up at me with her luminous eyes, sparkling with gold like some dazzling liqueur.

"I am not a fettered princess, but a bitch, a genuine bitch, with an honest bitch's heart. I'm not responsible for my too conspicuous beauty, which has aroused your possessive instincts. Is that the sole reason for your buying me? Is it for my silver coat, my prow-shaped chest, the curved arc of my body which seems to drink in the air, my taut brittle bones barely covered by my light sparse flesh. My gait delights you, and also the harmonious leap in which I appear both to jump over and crown an invisible portico, and you call me chained princess, chimera, lovely serpent, fairy steed. . . . Yet here you stand dumbfounded! I am only a bitch, with the heart of bitch, proud, ill with suppressed tenderness and trembling for fear I may give myself too quickly. Yes, I am trembling, because you now have me, past redemption, for ever, in exchange for those few drops of water poured by your hand, every night, into the bottom of a chipped basin."

MOMENTS OF STRESS

Is it today he'll kill himself?

There he goes, bunched on his bicycle, back humped like a snail, nose between his knees, swaying as he pedals on the revolving platform, struggling, as though in the teeth of a gale, against its centrifugal force.

The rimless tray spins beneath him, slowly at first, then faster, till it becomes at full speed a polished shimmering disk of watered silk, scored with concentric circles, like ripples when a pebble is dropped in a fountain. Upon its surface the small black figure astride two wheels pits his strength against the unceasing repulsion of the invisible force and, when he begins to falter, each lapse wrings from us one and all a similar strangled gasp.

The whole contraption sweeps round to the muffled roar of its motor; the deadly edges of the turn-table crackle with electric sparks, green and red; a siren maintains a shrill, agonising wail throughout the race.

Despite the spiralling blast that sweeps over the stage, we stay there, all of us, hidden in the wings; mute, competent mechanics in boiler suits; acrobats with their hair greased, their faces the pink of artificial flowers; small part actresses in hastily flung on faded kimonos, hair scraped back Chinese fashion under their filthy rubber 'make-up bands'. We stay there, all of us, glued to the spot by the hideous excitement of the unspoken query, "Is it today he'll ride to his death?"

No. It's all over now. The chromatic keening of the siren is silenced the moment the dizzy speed slackens to a standstill, and the black insect, after battling against odds gripped to the handlebars, alights with an elastic leap on to the now motionless disk.

No, it won't be today he'll kill himself. Unless, of course, this evening. . . . For today is Sunday, and this is only the first house. Clearly, therefore, he still has the time to kill himself at the evening performance.

I would like to get out of this place. But outside rain is falling, the depressing, black and desolate rain of the south, which has turned a whole town—white in the sun yesterday the length of its sea front—into a yellow quagmire. Outside this place there is only the rain and the hotel bedroom. Those who travel without respite, those who wander in isolation, those who sit down in a small restaurant at a table laid with a single plate, a single glass, and prop their folded newspaper against the water jug, such persons know the periodic, regular recurrence of fits of mental despair, the disease bred of loneliness.

I would like to get away from here, but for the moment I lack the strength to carry out my wish or to imagine any place that might bring me comfort. To create such a place, or revive it in my memory, to liven it with a beloved face, with flowers, streams, domestic animals, is for the present too great an effort, but it may be granted me a little later, perhaps in an hour's time. My mental inertia adapts itself to the physical lassitude which holds me here, faint-hearted and with sagging legs, querulously repeating to myself 'I would like to get away. . . .'

I fear, I expect some unknown tragedy. I am alarmed that the management has assembled here, for the perverse pleasure of an alien audience accustomed to view with indifference the spilling of the dark blood of bulls, so many dangerous or macabre "acts". A slight fever make my temples throb—journey-fatigue, change of climate, saline humidity?—transmagnifying, perhaps, familiar, almost friendly scenery into the trappings of a romantic nightmare. Tonight my peculiar mood isolates me from my bespangled and needy brethren who bustle about all round me; myself invisible, I watch their act from a sort of elevated quay, round which runs an iron balcony connecting the dressing-rooms and overlooking the stage.

A red demon has just this moment sprung from a trap-door and I can hear the laughs he raises among the distant public by his little pointed red beard and forked eyebrows, indeed by his entire mask, modelled in thick plaster and heavily black pencilled.

But the man has begun his labours as a contortionist, a

slow, serpentine dislocation, the unscrewing of each articulation, a double-jointed entanglement of every limb knit into an involved, uncanny pattern, and from up here I can see why it is he hides his features beneath those of a laughable demon: his self-inflicted tortures are such that at times his face refuses to obey him and really does become that of a man condemned to everlasting flames. Will he succumb, like a reptile strangled by its own coils? What is more, he is my side of the orchestra, and the music fails to drown his frequent moans, the brief involuntary moans of a man being slowly crushed to death.

When at last he goes off and passes, limping, below me, dragging his long body that looks half drained of its strength, I expand my constricted chest, I want to breathe. I trust this is the last of those brief horrors, I long for some insipid flowery ballet . . . but already the rifles are being levelled at their target, an ace of clubs held aloft in the hand of a trusting child.

I cannot endure the sight of this small hand, and in my morbid state I imagine its palm pierced by a red hole. Yet even so I remain, I even approach a little closer, returning to cower behind a stay, fascinated by a flight of navaja blades hurled at lightning speed by a knife-thrower. The man seems hardly to move, a flash of blue steel darts from his fist to penetrate, vibrating, a vertical board and are to be seen planted close against the temples of a youth, who wears a fixed smile and never bats an eyelid.

I myself blink as each blade passes and, each time, I lower my head. A scream from the audience, the cry of a frightened woman, finally shatters my nerves, but the youth is still there, and alive, smiling and petrified. Nothing has happened; he is alive, alive! Nothing has happened but the suspension, no doubt, the temporary indecision—for an immeasurably short instant—of whatever was hovering over this theatre. A sovereign wing, one that did not deign to descend today, has spared the man on the revolving table, spared the tortured neck of the red demon. It has not chosen to divert from their mark the bullets aimed at the ace of clubs held on high by a frail hand. Yet, for a split second, it remained poised, capriciously, above the head of the youthful Saint Sebastian who is smiling, down there, his brow haloed with knives.

Now it has resumed its flight. Will it fly far from us, this Fate whose invisible presence has so painfully oppressed me and left me with so trembling a soul, pusillanimous and greedy for horrors, the soul of a theatre-addict?

JOURNEY'S END

"Well I never! Who'd 'ave thought our paths would ever cross again! How long is it now since I last set eyes on you! Why, Marseilles of course, remember? You were on tour with the Pitard Company, and I with the Dubois. We both played the same night. It was up to our lot not to be done down by yours, and vice versa. That didn't stop us going out to have a bite together that night, shell fish, eh! on the terrace, at Basso's.

" . . . No, you've not changed much, I must say. You've looked after number one all right; you're lucky! Your digestion's been your saving, but if you've got thirteen years of touring in your system, like me, you wouldn't be looking so nifty!

"Yes, go ahead, you can tell me I've changed! At forty-six, it's a bit hard having to play duenna parts, when there are so many skittish youngsters of fifty and sixty to be seen footling about in juvenile leads on the Grands Boulevards, who'll throw up their parts, as likely as not, if there's a brat of over twelve in the cast! It was Saigon knocked me out, and long before my time too. I sang in operetta at Saigon, I did, in a theatre lit by eight hundred oil lamps!

" . . . And what else? Well, apart from that, there's not much to tell. I go on "touring", like so many others. I keep saying I've had enough of it, and this'll be the last time I'll do it; I go on saying to all who'll listen that I'd rather be a theatre attendant or travel in perfumery. So what? Here I am back again with Pitard, and you're back with Pitard too. We came back to find work, and it's noses to the grindstone once again.

" . . . I don't need you to tell me that prices have dropped all round. If it got about what I'm working for this time, my reputation would be gone. It really seems as if they think we don't need to eat when on tour.

"Not to mention that I've got my sister with me, you know. It may make two on the pay-roll but it means two mouths to feed. Oh, she's taken to the life right enough, the poor kid; she's got guts! More guts than health, if you ask me! She'll tackle any part. Take the time when we had a fifty-day contract with the Miral Touring Company, in a mixed bill of three plays nightly: the child took the part of the maid who lays the table in the first—ten lines; then an old peasant woman who tells everyone a few home truths—two hundred lines; and to end up, a girl of seventeen married off against her will who never stops crying throughout. Just think of the poor thing having to cope with all those changes of make-up!

"And for starvation fees, too, I'd have you know! On top of that we had the doctor's and chemist's bills to pay —it was the winter my bronchitis was so bad—not to mention the nurse's charge for cupping, thirty-seven francs worth! I went on rehearsing with forty cups on my back and so hid the fact I was suffering. When I was seized by a fit of coughing, I rushed off to the lav, otherwise they'd have replaced me within the hour, you bet!

"I was able to get away, but doctors and their drugs had ruined me in advance. It was then the child began to knit woollen garments, you know, those loose coatees that are fashionable just now, with a little woollen jumper to match. She works when we're travelling, on the train; she's got the knack of it. When we're in for a journey, eight or nine hours by rail, she'll reel off a coatee in four days and post it off at once to a firm in Paris.

" . . . Yes, yes, I know, you've got the music-hall to keep you going. There's still a living to be made on the halls; but what d'you suppose there's left for me? They'll bury my bones on one of these tours and, believe me, I'm not the only one. . . . Oh, I'm not trying to plead constant illness, you know. I still have my good moments; I was happy-go-lucky enough when young! If only my liver let me alone for three weeks, or if my cough left off for a fortnight, or the blessed varicose veins didn't make my left leg weigh so heavy, then I'd be my old self again!

"If, granted that, I chanced on a few good companions, not too mangy a lot, but sporty, who don't spend their lives harping on their woes and retailing their maladies and confinements, then I promise you I'd soon get my fair share of fun again.

"Provided, of course, I'm not laid out like Marizot. . . .

didn't you know? It wasn't in the papers, but the story
might have come your way. We were . . . now, where
were we? . . . in Belgium, in pouring rain. We'd just
finished a passable dinner, that is, my sister and I,
Marizot and Jacquard. Marizot goes out first, while we
stay behind to settle the bill. You know how short-sighted
he is. He misses his way, and off he goes down a dark
narrow street, and there at the end was a stream, a river,
I don't know, the Scheldt, or something: to be brief, he
falls into the water and gets carried away. They only
found him two days later. It all happened so quick that
the first night after, we hadn't even begun to feel sad
believe me! It wasn't till the next night, when the under-
manager played Marizot's part, that we all began to get
weepy and cried on the stage . . .

"Anyhow, people don't drown every day, thank God!
We did find some consolation at the time of the railway
strike. Yes, and it played us a most unusual trick. Listen
to this: we ended up the tour with *Fiasco*—the devil of a
title—and the night before we'd played it in Rouen. When
we reach Mantes, the train stops. 'All change! Everyone to leave the train! We go no further!' The strike
was on! Off I went to have a good moan. I had acute
liver trouble, rheumatism in my left leg, a high tempera-
ture, the whole boiling. I sat down on a bench in the
waiting-room, saying to myself, 'After a knock like this
nothing will get me to budge again, my luck's right out,
I'd rather die on the spot!' Jacquard was there, same as
ever, with his big overcoat and his pipe, and he comes up
to me and says 'Why don't you just go home. You'd
better take the Pigalle-Halle-aux-vins bus, which drops
you on your doorstep.'

" 'Oh, leave me in peace!' I give him for answer.
'Have you no heart at all? Here we are, stuck for Lord

knows how long by this filthy strike? D'you think I get much fun out of spending my miserable salary on drugs and digs, eh! I'd like you to be standing in my shoes and then see what you'd do in my place!'

" 'In your place?' he says. 'In your place I'd take the Pigalle-Halle-aux-vins bus.'

"I could have cried with rage, dearie. I could have struck him, that Jacquard, with his pipe and his wooden mug! I flayed him alive with my tongue! When I'm finished, he takes me by the arm and forcibly leads me to the glass door. And what d' you suppose I see in the station yard? *Pigalle-Halle-aux-vins*, dearie! *Pigalle,* in so many words! Three Pigalle buses, that had been used to bring along another troupe that very morning! And there they were, having a soft drink, right in front of that station at Mantes!

"I started to giggle, not but what my liver was killing me, and on I giggled till I thought I never would stop. And the best of it was that we went back to Paris in *Pigalle-Halle-aux-vins*, dearie, by the special authority of the sub-prefect. It cost us a bit more than two and a half francs, but what a time we all had! Jacquard and Marval sat on the top deck and threw down sausage skins to us inside, and you should have seen the faces of the 'by-standers'! That alone was worth the whole trip!

"And what a shaking we had, I felt as if my liver were being torn from my body at every jolt! It might well have been worse, for I laughed the whole length of the way, and that's always something to the good!

"And, when all's said and done, as Jacquard put it, 'What are speed and altitude records to the likes of us? Give me a nice little bus-ride *Mantes-Paris* on a *Pigalle-Halle-aux-vins* every time! There's an endurance test quite out of the ordinary!"

"THE STRIKE, OH LORD, THE STRIKE!"

THROUGH half-closed eyes I follow the "Pavane" as
danced by "The Great Concubines of History". Previous
to wearing the pearly-veiled hennin, the starched ruff,
the farthingale, the hooped panniers and knotted kerchief,
they have, for the rehearsal, pinned up their skirts like
loin-cloths about their hips, some even discarding their
narrow dresses to work in black knickers, bare arms
emerging from their brassiere, furry mob-caps on their
heads.

They are led by the Roi-Soleil, in the guise of a ballet-
master in shirt sleeves. Gabrielle d'Estrées and the Marquise de Pompadour persist in making mistake after mistake, and inwardly I bless them. They start over again
from the beginning. If only they would go on making
mistakes!

Seated in the orchestra stalls on a strip of grey dust-
sheet, I am waiting in the darkened auditorium till the
Revue rehearsal is over. It is now a quarter to six, my
comrades have held the stage since twelve-thirty. There'll
only be three-quarters of an hour left to rehearse our
mimodrama piece. But I long for Gabrielle d'Estrées and
the Marquise de Pompadour to blunder again: I do so
hate the thought of having to move.

The niggard gleam of a two-way "service lamp" acts
as substitute for the footlights. These two points of light,
hanging in the blackness, prick my eyes and induce sleep.
Beside me, invisible, a fellow mime staves off his craving
to smoke by chewing an unlit cigarette. "Another day's
work ruined for the rest of us! I should like to see all
Revue promoters deep in a hundred feet of . . . Just take

a look at those "Great Concubines", I ask you! And to think that they're toiling away there for the price of air. . . . The strike, oh Lord, the strike!"

The word arouses me. Is the strike, then, a reality? We've been talking about it so much among ourselves. There's been some change of atmosphere in this hard-worked Café-Concert of ours, one of the happiest establishments in the district, always warm and packed to capacity, where, every night, the stormy laughter of the crowd rollicks round the house amid cat-calls, whistling and stamping of feet.

"The strike, oh Lord, the strike!"

It's in the thoughts of all, it's mooted in corners. The chorus girls of the forthcoming Revue, the little singing girls on tour, have this word only on their lips, each in her own manner. Some there are who shout in a whisper "The Strike—for paid matinées, and paid rehearsals!", their faces afire, brandishing a muff like a flag and a reticule like a sling.

Once again the "Great Concubines" have gone agley. Splendid, a further ten good minutes in my seat! My Ladies de Pompadour and d'Estrées are "getting it in the neck"! Bending over them, the ballet-master lets fly a string of not very strong oaths which the Vert-Galant's mistress, a short, well-rounded brunette, receives with impatience, facing in our direction, her eyes on the exit.

The other, the Marquise, hangs her head like a child who has broken a vase. She stares at the floor, without saying a word; her breath lifts the heavy lock of blonde hair that falls across her cheek. The dismal light beating down from above sculpts her head into that of a thin, hollow-cheeked boy-martyr, and this Pompadour, in her black knickers with bare knees showing above her rolled stockings, bears a strange resemblance to a young

drummer-boy of the Revolution. Her whole stubborn
little hurt person spells rebellion and seems to cry aloud
"Long live the strike!"

At a standstill for the moment, the Pavane has re-
grouped round her, twenty silent young women at the
end of their tether. In the dark their eyes try to pick out
the seat from which the Manager supervises their movements, while they wait eagerly for the liberating words
"That will be all for today" to surge up from some dim
spot in the stalls. But they also appear tonight to be waiting for something else: "The strike, oh Lord, the strike!"
Tonight there is something aggressive about their
fatigue.

In direct contrast to the men—singers and mimes,
dancers and acrobats—who strive to preserve a serious
man-to-man tone, courteous and calm in discussion,
when they further their claims, the little "Caf'-Conc'"
girls, my comrades, have caught fire immediately. Being
emotional Parisiennes, the mention of the single word
"strike" makes them imagine confusedly mobs out in the
streets, riots, barricades.

The girls don't make a practice of it. The strict and
simple discipline by which we are ruled brooks no
infringement. Under the bluish sun of two projectors has
been evolved, up till these troubled days, the most
rigorous and hard-worked routine for small communi-
ties, alleviated in a trice by a word from the Manager
"Take it easy, Ladies. Do you think you're in a theatre?"
or "I don't like people who bawl at me." Yes, they don't
make a habit of "refractoriness" or going on strike. That
Agnes Sorel over yonder, who stands so tall on her
long legs, yawning with hunger, will soon be off and away
to her pigeon-house, at the back of beyond on the other
side of the Butte de Montmartre. She never has the time

for a hot meal, she lives too far away, she's always on the trot.

"It's not per performance she earns her monthly hundred and eighty francs, but per mile!" says Diane de Poitiers, who wears thin summer blouses in mid-December.

As for that handsome Montespan of the heavy bosom, is it for a moment likely that she acquired her habitual complaints from her husband, a consumptive bookbinder! She has more than enough on her hands looking after her man and two kids far out near the Château-d'Eau district.

They are so easily regimented, these poor honeyless bees! Any milliner's apprentice in the Rue de la Paix could put them wise on the question of claims. They said in the past "Great! We strike!" as they would have said "We're going to win the big lottery!", without any conviction. Now that they do believe in it, they are beginning to tremble, with hope.

Will they receive full pay for those terrible twice-nightly performances on Sunday and Thursday, and for the fête-days sprinkled throughout the calendar? Even better: will they be compensated for the long prison-hours, midday to six, while a Revue is in production? Would the snack of croissants, bock and banana they bolt in rehearsal time be buckshee? And Old Mother Louis, our rheumaticky duenna, who plays comic mothers-in-law and negresses, will her bus-fare on Sundays and Thursdays be drawn from some other source than the miserable pin money she earns by her knitting, she who knits, everywhere and every minute, for a knitted garment shop?

As for those rush-hour nights, dreaded above all when the full-dress rehearsal for a Revue goes on till dawn, would it no longer be solely "for the honour of the house" that fifty or so "walkers" from the chorus have to go back home in the freezing early hours, . . . swollen feet and weak ankles, yawning themselves to death?

It sounds good. It is disquieting. Our little community is at fever-pitch. At night, in the wings, someone seizes me by the sleeves, and questions me.

"You're for the strike, aren't you?" and someone else adds, in a voice of assurance but with fluttering gestures, "In the first place, it's only fair."

Not everybody shares the bitter scepticism of this blonde, hollow-cheeked child, Mme de Pompadour, a philosopher of nineteen, whom I have nicknamed Cassandra and who resents it without exactly knowing why. "If we strike, where will it get us? It will only help to fatten the cinema crowd. And while it lasts, what are the two of us going to feed on, Moman and me?"

It must be at least a quarter past six. I am almost asleep, my arms pushed deep in my muff, my chin in my fur. I feel warm on the shoulders and cold in the feet, due to the fact that the central heating is not lit for rehearsals. What am I doing here? It is too late for work today. I have gone on waiting with the fatalistic patience learned in the music-hall. I may as well wait on a little longer and then leave at the same time as the tired swarm of day girls who will disperse over the face of Paris.

The ones in the greatest hurry and those whose job brings them back here at eight, will not go far afield: the slice of pale veal on its bed of sorrel, or the dubious lamb stew, await them in the brasserie round the corner. The others make off at the run as soon as their feet touch the pavement. "I've just time to rush home for a minute."

Rush home to a grumbling "Moman", for a wash and

clean, to retie the ribbon that binds hair and forehead, to make sure that the kid has not fallen from the window or burnt himself on the stove, and houpla! the return journey. They jump on a bus, a tram, the underground, pell mell with all the other employees—milliners, seamstresses, cashiers, typists—for whom the day's work is over.

BASTIENNE'S CHILD

I

"Run, Bastienne, run!"

The ballerinas scurry the whole length of the corridor, brushing the petals of their skirts against the wall, leaving behind them the smell of rice powder, hair still warm from the curling-tongs, new tarlatan gauze. Bastienne runs, not quite so fast, both hands encircling her waist. They have been "rung" rather late, and were she to arrive on the stage out of breath, might she not fumble, perhaps, the end of her variation, that lengthy spin during which nothing is seen of her but the fully extended, creamy swirl of a ballet-skirt and two slim pink legs moving apart and coming together again with a mechanical precision already appreciated by connoiseurs?

She is not, as yet, anything more than a very young dancer, under a year's contract to the Grand-Théâtre at X; a poor girl, of radiant beauty, tall, "expensive to feed" as she says of herself, and underfed, because she is already five months pregnant.

Of the child's father, there is no news.

"He's a bad lot, that man!" says Bastienne.

But she speaks of him without tearing out her dark hair, so silky against her clear white skin, and her "misfortune" has not driven her either to the river, or to the gas oven. She dances as before and recognises three powerful deities: the manager of the Grand-Théâtre, the ballet-mistress, and the proprietor of the hotel where live, besides Bastienne herself, a dozen of her comrades. However, since the morning when Bastienne, turning deathly pale during the dancing lesson, confessed with a peasant's simplicity "Madame, it's because I'm expecting!" the ballet-mistress has spared her. But she does not wish to be spared, and dismisses any special attention with an indignant jerk of the elbow and a "Why, I'm not ailing!"

The weight that swells her waist-line she calmly accepts, apart from passing a few rude remarks on it with the inconsequence of her seventeen years. "As for you, I'm going to put some sense in you!" And she pulls in her belt, loath not to display for as long as possible, and above all on the stage, the flexibility of her slim, broad-shouldered figure. She laughingly insults her burden, slapping it with the flat of her hands, then adding "How hungry it makes me!" Unthinkingly she commits the heroic imprudence of all penniless girls: having paid her weekly hotel bill, she often goes to bed without dinner or supper, and keeps her stays on all night to "cut her appetite".

Bastienne, in fact, leads the indigently, happy-go-lucky but hard-working life of the little motherless ballerinas who have no lover. Between the morning lesson, starting at nine, the afternoon rehearsal, and the nightly performance, they have next to no time left for thought. Their wretched phalanstery does not know the meaning of despair, since solitude and insomnia never afflict its members.

Impudent and crafty after their fashion, driven to extremes by the ragings of an empty stomach, Bastienne and her room-mate—a dumpy little blonde—sometimes spend their last pennies in the Grand-Théâtre Brasserie, after midnight, on a bottle of beer.

Seated opposite one another, they shrilly exchange the remarks of a prearranged dialogue.

"Now, if I had the money, I'd treat myself to a fat ham-sandwich!"

"Yes, but you've not got a sou. I've got none neither, but supposing I had, I'd certainly order myself a nice grilled black pudding, with lots of mustard and a hunk of bread. . . ."

"Oh, I'd far rather have a sauerkraut, with plenty of sausage. . . ."

It so happens that the sauerkraut and the grilled black pudding, so feverishly evoked, providentially descend between the two little ballerinas, escorted by the generous donor, whom they welcome with thanks, with a joke and a smile, and then leave in the lurch, all before the half hour has struck.

This innocent method of begging is the invention of Bastienne, whose "interesting condition" earns her a curiosity not so far removed from consideration. Her comrades count the weeks and consult the cards concerning the child's fortune. They make a fuss of her, helping to tighten her dancing stays with a heave-ho as they pull on the lace, one knee pressed against her robust thighs. They freely bestow on her preposterous advice, recommending her to take witch's potions, ever helpful, and shouting after her, as tonight, down the long dark corridors, "Run, Bastienne, run!"

They keep an anxious eye on her imprudent dancing, insist above all on escorting her back to her dressing-room, to be there at the moment when, unhooking her torturous breastplate, she laughingly threatens the youngest, silliest, and most inquisitive with "Take care, or he'll pop out and perch on your nose!"

Today, in the warmest corner of the big dressing-room, there stands, supported on two chairs, the tray of an old travelling-trunk with a canopy of flowered wallpaper. It is the piteous crib of a tiny little Bastienne, hardy as a weed. She is brought to the theatre by her mother at eight, and is removed at midnight under her cloak. This much-dandled, merry little mite, this babe with scarcely a stitch of clothing, who is dressed by small clumsy hands that knit for it, awkwardly, pilches and bonnets, enjoys, despite her environment, the gorgeous childhood of a fairy-tale princess. Ethiopian slaves in coffee-coloured tights, Egyptian girls hung with blue jewellery, houris stripped to the waist, bend over her cot and let her play with their necklaces, their feather fans, their veils that change the colour of the light. The tiny little Bastienne falls asleep and wakes in scented young arms, while Peris, with faces the rose pink of fuchsias, croon her songs to the rhythm of a far distant orchestra.

A dusky Asian maid, keeping watch by the door, shouts down the corridor, "Run, Bastienne, run! Your daughter is thirsty!"

In comes Bastienne, breathless, smoothing her tense billowing skirts with the tips of her fingers, and runs straight to the tray of the old travelling trunk. Without waiting to sit down or unfasten her low-cut bodice, she uses both hands to free from its pressure a swollen breast, blue in colour from its generous veins. Leaning over, one foot lifted in the dancer's classical pose, her flared skirts like a luminous wheel around her, she suckles her daughter.

II

"Look, Bastienne, the Serbs are here, and over here is Greece. This part streaked with thin lines is Bulgaria. All this bit marked in black shows the advance made by the Allies, while the Turks have been forced to retreat as far as here. Now d'you understand?"

Bastienne's huge eyes, the colour of light tobacco, are wide open and she nods her head politely, muttering "Mmm . . . Mmm . . ." She takes a long look at the map over which her companion Peloux is running a thin, hardened finger, and finally exclaims "Lord, how small it is, how very small!"

Peloux, who was hardly expecting this conclusion, bursts out laughing, and it is on her now that Bastienne focuses in astonishment her huge orbs, always a little slow in registering any change of thought.

The complicated map, covered with dotted lines and hatching, represents to Bastienne nothing but a confused design for embroidery. Fortunately Constantinople is there, printed in capitals. She knows of its existence, it's a town. Peloux has a sister, an elder sister of twenty-eight, who once played in a comedy at Constantinople, in the presence of . . .

"In whose presence was it, Peloux, your sister played in Constantinople?"

"In front of the Sultan, of course!" comes the lie direct from Peloux.

Bastienne, incredulous and deferential, spends another moment or two deciphering the newspaper. What a lot of unreadable names! What a lot of unknown countries! For, after all, she did once dance in a *Divertissement* which brought together the five parts of the world. Very well, those five parts were: America, which had meant a foundation make-up of terra cotta; Africa, nigger-brown tights; Spain, fringed shawls; France, a snow-white tutu, and for Russia red leather boots. If the map of the world had now to be cut up like a jigsaw puzzle, and from each small section had to be conjured up a fully armed, wicked little nation nobody had ever heard of, then it made life far too complicated. . . . Bastienne casts a hostile glance at the nebulous photographs round the edge of the map and declares "To start with, all those chaps there look like the cycle cops in their flat caps! Now, Peloux, supposing you give the child a good slap, just to teach her not to eat your thread!"

Tired of staring so long at 'small print', Bastienne gets to her feet, sighs, and winds round her ear, like a ribbon, a strand of her long black hair. She deigns to cast a majestic animal glance upon her daughter, crawling on all fours at her feet, then bends down and, lifting a corner of the petticoat and chemise, administers by the count, on a round rosy little behind, a good half dozen resounding slaps.

"Oh!" protests Peloux, in rather a frightened whisper.

"Don't you worry," Bastienne retorts, "I'm not killing her. Besides, she minds pain so little, it's unbelievable."

Indeed, there's no sound to be heard either of the dramatic tears or the piercing shrieks of very young children when they sob to the point of suffocation: nothing but the furious drubbing of two small shoes against the floor boards where the tiny little Bastienne rolls herself into a ball like a caterpillar knocked off a gooseberry bush, and no more.

. . . Bastienne is today a truly magnificent creature, due to her premature motherhood, and to having recovered the habit of regular meals now that she has a warm lodging. A gallant tradesman, as much out of pity as dazzled by her beauty, had brought home mother and child on Christmas Eve when Bastienne was revelling on tuppence worth of hot roasted chestnuts.

His reward is to come back every evening to the small apartment from which can be seen a grey flowing river and find there a tall, friendly Bastienne, gay, a little standoffish but faithful, busied over her career and her daughter. She thrives in a home of her own, at ease in one of those aprons such as are worn by girls who deliver bread, and tied, as it is today, over her kimono, her hair hanging over her shoulders with that newly washed but still uncombed look that enhances her nineteen years.

This is a lovely holiday afternoon for Bastienne and her friend Peloux. No ballet is in rehearsal at the Grand-Théâtre, the dry December weather makes the stove roar, and ahead of them lie four good hours of freedom, while drop by drop the coffee fills the tinplate filter. Peloux is puckering the 'underskirts' of a work-a-day costume in coarse bluish-white tarlatan and, without pricking her finger or making a mistake, she contrives to keep an eye on the war news, the deserted street, and a catalogue of novelties.

"You know, Bastienne, we won't have any more roasted pistachio-nuts, on account of the war: that old Turk who sells them told me as much. . . . That's the third time that lieutenant down there has repassed the house. . . . Bastienne, what about an astrakan cloak like this one here, when you're rich? You'd look stunning in it!"

But Bastienne's placid soul, her stay-at-home, domesticated little dancer's soul, yearns for no furs. When she goes window-shopping, her eye lingers on unbleached linen rather than on velvets, and she lets her fingers run over rough scarlet-bordered dusters. . . . At present she is smiling in an honestly sensuous way over her favourite chore: standing over a small basin, her lovely arms covered in lukewarm froth, looking as beautiful as a queen in a wash-house, she is soaping her daughter's underwear, without spilling a drop around her. . . . Why could not life, her future, that is, and even her duty, be contained within the four gaily papered walls of this small dining-room, scented with coffee, white soap and orris-root? Life, for a now flourishing though once misery-racked Bastienne, means dancing in the first place, then working, in the humble and domestic sense of the word given it by the race of thrifty females. Jewellery, money, fine clothes . . . these are things not so much rejected by stern choice, as postponed by Bastienne. They lie somewhere faraway in her thoughts, and she does not call them forth. One day they may just happen, like a legacy, like a chimney-pot falling on your head, or like the arrival of the mysterious little daughter now playing on the floor-rug, whose healthy growth still gives Bastienne a daily increasing awareness of the miraculous and unforeseen.

A year ago everything in life had seemed simple: to suffer hunger and cold, to have leaky shoes, to feel lonely and miserable and heavily burdened in body, "all that might well happen to anyone" Bastienne had blandly remarked. All was simple then, and still is, except for the existence of her fifteen-month-old child, except for the blonde little angel, curly-headed and up to every trick, now in a silent rage on the floor-rug. To so young and inexperienced a mother, a child is a lovely warm little creature, dependant, according to its age, on milk, soup, kisses and slaps. So things go on and on until . . . good heavens, until the time comes for the first dancing-class. But it so happens that before her very eyes, under her warm kisses and stinging smacks, a small being is fast developing an independent personality, thinking, struggling, and arguing even before knowing how to talk! And that, Bastienne had not foreseen. 'A chit of fifteen months, who already has ideas of her own!'

Peloux shakes her head with the earnest, pinched expression that gives her at twenty an old maidish look, and starts to tell stories of infant prodigies and criminal children. The truth is that the surprising little Bastienne, aged fifteen months, already knows how to captivate, fib, make pretence of tummy-ache, or, sobbing loudly, stretch out a plump hand nobody has trodden on; knows, too, the power of obstinate silence, and above all knows how to pretend to be listening to the grown ups' conversation, eyes wide open, mouth tight shut, so much so that Peloux and Bastienne sometimes behave like frightened schoolgirls and suddenly stop talking, because this disturbing witness, with its mop of fair curls, looks less like a baby than a mischievous little Eros.

It is on the face of the tiny little Bastienne, far more than on her mother's lovely tranquil face or Peloux's already faded features, that are mirrored all the worldly passions: uncontrolled coveteousness, dissimulation, beguiling seductiveness.

"Oh, how peaceful we should be," sighs Peloux, "were it not for this magpie of a child gobbling up all my needles."

"Catch her, if you can leave your stitching," Bastienne answers. "My hands are covered with suds."

But the "magpie of a child" has parked itself behind the sewing-machine, and all that can be seen, between the treadle and the platform, is a pair of deep blue eyes, which, in their isolation, might be fifteen months, or fifteen years, or older still.

"Come here, you delicious lump of poison!" Peloux begs.

"Will you come here, you fiend incarnate!" Bastienne scolds.

No answer. The blue eyes move only an instant to cast their insolent light on Bastienne. And if Peloux redoubles her entreaties and Bastienne her invective, it will not be from fear that the fair chubby-cheeked Eros ambushed behind the sewing-machine may devour a gross of needles; it will be rather to hide the constraint, the embarrassment imposed on outspoken grown ups when under scrutiny from a small unfathomable child.

CHEAP-JACKS

THE ACCOMPANIST

"MADAME BARUCCHI is on her way, Madame, please don't be impatient with her: she's just telephoned to say she can't help being a little late for your lesson, on account of the dress rehearsal of the ballet at the Empyrée. You have a few minutes to spare, I'm sure."

" . . . "

"In any case, we're a little fast in here, it's only ten to . . . When I say 'we', well, I'm always on time myself. I hardly ever move from here the whole day long."

" . . . ?"

"No, it's not that the work is really hard; but it is sometimes a little dreary in this large, bare studio. And then, in the evening, I must say I do feel a bit tired in the back from sitting on the piano-stool.

" . . . "

"So young? But I'm not so young, I'm twenty-six! Sometimes I feel so old, from doing the same thing day after day! Twenty-six, a little boy of five, and no husband."

" . . . ?"

"Yes, he was mine, that little boy you saw yesterday. When he comes out from his nursery-school, Mme Barucchi is kind enough to let me have him here, so that I don't have to fret about what's become of him. He's sweet. He watches all these ladies here at their lesson, he's learnt a few steps already. He's an observant child."

"   . . . "

"Yes, I know. I'm always being told that I'm doing an old woman's job and that I can well afford the time to wait until I'm grey-haired before settling down as an accompanist, but I'd rather stick where I am. And then I've already suffered a good many hard knocks in my life, so all I ask is to be left to sit quietly on my piano-stool. . . . You're looking at the time? Be patient for a little longer! Mme Barucchi can't be long now. I know you're wasting precious minutes, whereas I'm earning my income, at the moment, by twiddling my thumbs. That doesn't happen to me very often!"

"   . . . ?"

"Because I'm paid by the hour. Two francs fifty."

"   . . . !"

"You don't think that a lot? But just consider, Madame, everyone plays the piano, there's a neighbour of mine who gives lessons in town at a franc a time: out of that she has to pay her bus fare, plus the wear and tear of her shoe-leather and umbrella. And here am I under cover all day, and warm, even too warm: the studio stove sometimes makes me feel dizzy. But then I have the satisfaction of being among artistes; that makes up for a lot."

"   . . . ?"

"No, I've never been on the stage. I was a model once, before I had my little boy. That left me with certain tastes, certain habits. I could never again live a common or garden life. There was a moment, three years ago, when Mme Barucchi advised me to try the music-hall, as a dancer. . . . 'But', I said to her, 'I don't know how to dance.'—'That makes no difference,' she answered, 'you

could go on as a "dancer in the nude": then you wouldn't
tire yourself out by dancing.' I had no wish to do
that."

" . . . ?"

"Oh, that wasn't the only reason. A dancer in the nude,
as the saying goes, displays no more than any of the
others. A dancer in the nude always means something in
the Egyptian style, and that entails a good ten pounds'
weight of beaten-metal straps and belts and ornaments,
beaded lattice-work on the legs, necklaces from here to
there, and no end of veils. No, it wasn't merely the
question of decency that made me decline. It's my nature
to stay in my corner and watch the others.

"People are passing through here all day long, not only
the ladies of the music-hall, but actresses, real stage-
actresses, who play in the boulevard theatres, especially
now that there is so much dancing in straight plays. I
must admit they are like fish out of water at the start.
They're not accustomed to taking their clothes off for
their lesson. They arrive wearing the latest fashion
models, they begin by lifting up their dress and fastening
it with safety-pins, then they become exasperated, the
heat mounts higher, they unhook their collar, and then
they get rid of their skirt and next thing it's the blouse. . . .
Finally, their stays come off, hairpins start falling out and
some of their hair, too, on occasion, and their face-
powder turns moist. At the end of an hour's work you
would be in fits to see, in the place of a smart lady, an
ordinary little woman, running with sweat, who pants
and rages, swears a little, dabs her cheeks with a handkerchief, and doesn't care a button if her nose is shining:
in fact, just an ordinary woman! There's no malice in
what I've been saying, believe me, but it does amuse me.
I enjoy my little observations."

" . . . ?"

"Oh, certainly not, it gives me no wish to exchange my lot for theirs. The mere thought of such a thing makes me feel tired. Dancing lessons apart, they still go rushing around outside, at least that's how I see it. You should hear them retailing their grievances. 'Oh, heavens above, I have to be at such and such a place at five, and at my masseuse' at five-thirty, then back home for an appointment at six! Then there's my three stage dresses to try on! Oh, heavens above, I'll never get through it all!'

"It's terrifying. I have to close my eyes, they make me feel sleepy. The other day, for example, Mme Dorziat— yes, Mme Dorziat, in person—very kindly said to Mme Barucchi, referring to me, 'That poor girl, who's been grinding away at my dance-music for the last hour and a quarter, I shouldn't care to be in her place!' My place, my place, why, it's the one that suits me best! All I ask is to left alone in it. I fooled about a bit in my younger days, and I've been well punished for it! But it's left me apprehensive. The more I see of the way others fling themselves into the swirl of life, the more I want to remain seated. For here I see little else but the fuss and bother in which people become involved. Bright lights, spangles, costumes, painted faces, smiles, that spectacular sort of life is not for me. I see nothing but careers, sweat, skins that are yellow by the light of day, and despondency. . . . I'm not much good at expressing myself, but those are the lines along which my mind works. It seems as though I were the only person with a working knowledge of the sidelights that others view from the front of the stage."

" . . . ?"

"Get married, me? Oh, no, I should be afraid, now.

As I was saying, it's left me apprehensive. No, no, things are all right as they are, I wish to remain just as I am. Just as I am, with my little boy clinging to my skirts, both of us well sheltered behind my piano."

THE CASHIER

WATCH dogs, in a kennel with its back turned to the west wind, are better housed. She has her lair, from eight in the evening till midnight, and from two till five for matinées, in a damp recess under the stairs leading down to the artistes' dressing-rooms, and the battered little deal pay-desk is her sole protection against the brutal draught directed at her whenever the constantly opened and shut iron door swings back into place. Alternate hot and cold gusts, from the radiator on one side and the stairs on the other, slightly ruffle the curls round her head and her little knitted tippet, whose every stitch carries an imitation jet bead.

For the past twenty-four years she has been entering in a cash-book the number of soft drinks consumed in the stalls of the Folies-Gobelins, as well as those in the Café-Gobelins annexed to the theatre: bocks, mazagran coffees, brandied cherries. An electric bulb hangs above her head like a pear on a string, petticoated in green paper, and at first all that can be distinguished is a small yellow hand emerging from a starched cuff. A small yellow hand, clean, but with the thumb and forefinger blackened from counting coins and copper tallies.

After a short while of attentive scrutiny, the features of the cashier can easily be discerned, among the many green shadows cast by the lamp, on the shrivelled face of a pleasant, timorous old lizard, devoid of all colour. Supposing her cheek were pricked, would there spurt from it, instead of blood, pale globules of the anaemic juice used in bottling brandied cherries?

When I go down to my dressing-room, she hands me my key from on top of the five-shelved row of those special cherries for which the establishment is far famed: five cherries per portion in a glass cupel, arranged pyramidally, so that they look like the boxed shrubs in a French formal garden, with the ink-well, in this instance, a substitute for the glass-surfaced water.

I know nothing of the cashier except her bust, always bent forward from her habit of writing and her desire to please. . . . She arrives at the Folies-Gobelins long before me and leaves at midnight. Does she walk? has she legs and feet, a woman's body? All that must have melted away, after twenty-four years behind her battered little pay-desk!

A lizard, yes, a nice little wrinkled lizard, old and frail, but not so timorous after all: her tart voice has a shrill ring of authority, and to one and all alike she exhibits the equable kindliness of one whose power is undisputed. She treats the waiters like unruly children, tut-tutting like a governess, and the artistes like irresponsible or sick children, past correction. The chief stagehand, grey-haired, blue boiler-suited, speaks to her as would a small boy: he has been on the house staff for a mere eighteen years!

In some obscure way, the cashier feels herself to be as fixed and weather-beaten as the building itself, and the panel of her hutch, never whitewashed, never repainted, is thickly coated with a shiny black, with an indelible varnish of dirt: I can't help being reminded of other smoky traces left untouched by the centuries, the smoky traces of a lamp—for ever extinguished—at Cumae, in the Sibyl's cave.

It is from the lips of our benign Sibyl that I learn, in three words, whether the audience is dense or sparse, whether the trade in soft drinks is slack or flowing abundantly. She also informs me of how my face looks, of the temper of the upper gallery, and of the reception accorded to the evening's "first appearance".

I learn, into the bargain, that it is cold outside or that rain can be expected. What can she know of the weather, this cashier who, to reach her windswept hovel, must quit some other murky basement, far distant, and make her way by métro, under the ground, always under the ground.

Only smothered strains of the orchestra reach her, sometimes carrying on a wave of music the shrill high note of a popular soprano. . . . The applause crackles like a distant fall of rubble.

The cashier lends it her ear and says to me, "You hear them? All that is for little Jady! She's made quite a hit here. She's got a way of putting it across that is all her own, and she . . ."

Her voice sounds discreet, amiable; it remains for me to detect the underlying censure, the compassionate scorn for all things and creatures connected with the music-hall.

The cashier has great affection for the dirt and gloom of the Folies-Gobelins, for her hovel, her lamp with its green petticoat, and her flower borders of brandied cherries. What takes place on the stage is no concern of hers. When I rush off, out of breath, quite beside myself, and shout to her as I pass "How splendidly it's gone tonight, a first-rate audience! They made us take four curtain calls!" she smiles in response, and says "Now's the moment for you to rush to your dressing-room and give yourself a hard rub with eau-de-Cologne, or you'll catch a chill." She adds nothing but a superficial flicker of her keen eyes over my unfastened dress and my bare sandalled feet.

It is in the warmth and darkness of the Folies-Gobelins incubator that the insufferable little Jady was hatched out: two quivering legs, as clever and responsive as antennae, a pointed, fragile voice that breaks every other instant—like the legs of an insect, no sooner snapped than they've grown together again—and, the other day, when standing by the pay-desk, I happened to expatiate on the peculiar gifts of this singer born to be a dancer.

"Yes," the cashier concurred, "I'm bound to admit that she's won universal applause. They tell me she's got pep, she's got dash, she's got 'it', in other words, she's got everything, but how can I tell? But do you know her little girl? No? A darling, Madame, a real beauty! And so sweet and well mannered! Only two, but she knows how to say please and thank-you, and can even blow kisses! And amenable, too! You can leave her by herself at home the whole livelong day, just think of that!"

I do think of that. And I come to think that a despondent moralist, a discriminating if captious critic, is hidden away in this gloomy hovel under the stairs of the Folies-Gobelins. Our wrinkled Sibyl does not cry after us "Unhappy, erring folk that you are, have the words 'family', 'morals', 'hygiene', no meaning for you?" She smiles, rather, and murmurs at the end of a sentence which has no conclusion, "Think of that! . . ." And it needed no more than that for me to visualise, in some suburban tenement, a baby of two, *amenable*, left alone by itself all day, waiting contentedly until such time as its mother should finish her act.

NOSTALGIA

"Ir's me, Madame, it's the dresser. Has Madame everything she requires?"

" . . . !"

"Well! If this isn't something more than a surprise! I felt sure it would bowl you over to see me again! Yes, yes, it's me all right! You never expected to find your old Jeanne of the Empyrée-Clichy down here! Yes, I'm spending the winter in Nice, like the English. And how are things with you? All going well?"

" . . . "

"Same goes for me, not but what there's a deal I could say on the subject. . . ."

" . . . "

"Yes, yes, I'll get you dressed, never you worry. Now, for your first scene, is it this blue dress, or that tea-gown affair in pink?"

" . . . "

"Good! Once I know, I don't need telling a second time. Now, that is really something, that muslin with nothing under it. Very becoming. Why, it's the very spit of the costume little Miriam wore at the Empyrée, you remember?"

" . . . ?"

"Little Miriam, you surely remember, in the Apotheosis of Aviation, in this year's Spring Revue! And this one here does make a difference, as you might say, with the dress you wore at the Empyrée, don't it?"

" . . . ?"

"Why, the other winter. The peasant skirt, with the kerchief tied over your head, and clogs. My heart gave a

jump when I read your name on the posters here! I saw
you again as you were in your piece at the Empyrée; it
seemed like I was still there!"

" . . . ?"

"Me? Perish the thought! You have to have time on
your hands to feel proper fed up. My work's cut out for
me here, for it's me that has the cleaning of the dressing-
rooms. They've got no man to do the job, the theatre here
being so small! And matinée twice a week! And those
conferences, when I've got to be on the spot in case the
audition ladies need a stitch putting in here or a pin there.
. . . During the acts, yes, I must say it does get a bit
lonely like in the corridor; I get chilly, sitting there on
my chair. I doze off, and wake up thinking I'm still at
the Empyrée-Clichy. . . . Just think, when one's been
dresser for fifteen years in the same establishment! And
fifteen years of good service, I may say. Never a harsh
word did I have from Mme Barney, "the boss" as you
used to say. There's an able woman for you, Madame!
Hard on slackers, maybe, but above all fair. Naturally,
one spared oneself no pains when working for her. In
the last Revue, if you remember, I had sixteen ladies to
dress, eight on my passage, and eight on the landing, the
landing, you know, they had to convert into a dressing-
room for want of space. I'm not saying it turned out the
most suitable place: persons undressing don't much
care to see whoever it may be passing through at any
moment as they rush up and down the stairs. . . . Not
to mention the draughts. . . . Sixteen, I ask you! My
fingers were worn to the bone with all those hooks and
eyes. But there you are, Madame, never an entrance
missed!"

" . . . ?"

"But of course, I'm very happy here. What makes you

think I'm not? M. Lafougère is a very nice man. He's
engaged my son, as from tonight."

" . . . ?"

"Oh, no, not as an actor, you couldn't expect that! He
starts as a stagehand. That makes a pair of you making
your debut together like. It's for his health that I'm here.
The doctor says to me, he says: 'What he needs is the
south for his bronchial tubes.' M. Lafougère has taken
on the two of us."

" . . . ?"

"Oh, no, you won't be late. Precious little chance of
you ever being late here! A show billed for eight-thirty
may well start at nine, more or less. Ah, we're not with
Mme Barney no more! The music-hall, I always say, is
founded on punctuality."

" . . . ?"

"What's that noise you can hear? That's the actors in
the second piece, the one with the dancing. Listen to
them, just listen! And we shout, and we sing, tra-la-la,
and we pick quarrels! They've no manners, no self-
respect. No, but I ask you, do you hear them? With a
row like that, there's no more believing myself at the
Empyrée-Clichy. You've worked there yourself, so you
can tell me whether you ever heard one word spoken
louder than another in that house! The theatre and the
café-concert, it's not the same thing, whatever people may
say!"

" . . . "

"Oh, you can sigh, I don't blame you! Many's the time
I have to bite back my words not to give the ladies here
a piece of my mind. Only the other day one of them
yelled in my face "Keep the door shut, Jeanne, can't you,
when people are stark naked in their dressing-room. It's
plain to see you come from the music-hall!' Another

word, and I'd have answered back 'And it's plain to see that's where you don't come from. They've got no time for the likes of you! In the music-hall, we've no use for a skimpy cricket like you; what we want are persons who have the wherewithal to fill out their tights and their stays. . . .' Such words are best left unspoken: home truths are never popular. . . . Your little bronze shoes and stockings to match, do you want me to have them ready for the second play?"

" . . . !"

"Could be it's a Greek play; but you'll never find anything that sets off your legs to better advantage than bronze stockings and a pair of little shoes like these here. The main point about dancing is to set off one's legs. However, let us say I've never said a word. . . . You've never been back there again, to the old place?"

" . . . ?"

"But to the Empyrée-Clichy, of course! You don't know if my old colleague, Ma Martin, is still there?"

" . . . "

"So much the worst. I'd very much like to have news of her. She'd promised me faithfully to write, but envy must have turned her heart green. My engagement here has made many envious of me, you know. 'To Nice!' is what Ma Martin said to me, 'you're going to Nice! You are among the honoured! You'll be able to go over to Monte Carlo and win a fortune!'"

" . . . ?"

"No, I've not been there yet. But I'll go there all right! I'll go, if only to be able to tell them all at the old place that I have been there. I'll first tell Ma Martin, then I'll tell Mme Cavellier. . . ."

" . . . ?"

"Mme Cavellier, the romantic ballad singer, Rachel's sister!"

" . . . ?"

"Oh, yes, surely you do! Mme Cavellier, with a husband in the claque her sister, an American dancer, and her son a programme-seller in the foyer. Good Lord, aren't you forgetful now! I'd never have thought it of you! And Rita, don't you remember her? I knew it. Well, she's there no more."

" . . . ?"

"Where but at the Empyrée-Clichy, what do you expect?"

" . . . ?"

"What! Haven't I been talking to you of nothing but the Empyrée-Clichy? But what else would you have me talk of? Ah, but you're still a proper tease, I can see that! Don't chaff me unkindly, I have a real liking for you, because we were there together. And I can say this to you, for I know you won't laugh at me, but I read through, in yesterday's *Comœdia*, the full account of the Christmas Revue at the Empyrée-Clichy. Well, at the idea that they'd managed the whole thing without me— the rush and bustle of the dress rehearsal, the critic's preview, and the first night—why the paper dropped from my hands, and I began to cry like a silly old fool."

CLEVER DOGS

"HOLD her! Hold her! Oh, the bitch, she's nipped her again!"

Manette has just eluded the stagehand's grip and

hurled herself on Cora, who was half expecting it. But the little fox terrier is endowed with the speed of a projectile and her teeth have bitten right through the collie's thick fur and into the flesh of the neck. Cora does not retaliate at once; her ears intent on the curtain bell, her pendulous lips drawn back as far as her eyes, she offers no other threat to her comrade than a grimace as fierce as a vixen's mask and a strangled rattle, soft as the purring of a large cat.

Back in her master's arms, with the hair all down her back on end like pig's bristles, Manette is choking to say something offensive.

"They'd like to gobble each other up!" the stagehand remarks.

"The idea!" Harry retorts. "They're too conscientious for that. Quick, the collars."

While he is tying round Cora's neck the blue ribbon which sets off to advantage her fair coat, the colour of ripe wheat, the stagehand fastens on Manette's back a pug's harness of green velvet studded with gold, heavy with plaques and jingle-bells.

"Hold her tight, just long enough for me to get into my dolman. . . ."

Harry's snuff-coloured cardigan, brown with sweat, disappears beneath his sapphire blue dolman, padded round the shoulders and almost skin tight. Cora, restrained by the stagehand, gasps ever more loudly, keeping her eyes trained upwards on Manette's posterior, on a Manette almost in convulsions and quite terrifying, with her bloodshot eyes and backward cockled ears.

"Wouldn't a good dressing down quiet 'em?" ventures the boy in the blue jacket.

"Never before their act," Harry snaps categorically.

Behind the lowered curtain, he tests the equilibrium of

the railings which enclose the track of miniature obstacles, makes certain the platform and hurdle are secure, and polishes with a woollen rag the nickel-plated bars of the springboards on which the yellow collie will rebound. It is he too who goes to fetch from his dressing-room a set of paper hoops still damp from hasty resticking.

"I do everything myself!" he declares. "The master's eye. . . ."

Behind his back the stagehand shrugs his shoulders, "The master's eye, my foot! That means no tip for the team!"

The two-man "team" bears Harry no grudge on his fifteen francs a day takings. "Fifteen francs for three mouths and ten paws, that's not much!" the stagehand concedes.

Three mouths, ten paws and two hundred kilos of luggage. The whole concern tours throughout the year with the aid of special third-class half-fare rates. The year before there was an extra "mouth", that of the white poodle now defunct; an over-age old campaigner, a dog that had had his day, well-known in every French and foreign establishment, and much regretted by Harry, who loves to sing the praises of poor old Charlot.

"He knew how to do everything, Madame: waltz, somersault, spring-board work, all the tricks of a canine calculator, he knew the lot. He could have taught me a few, I'm telling you, and I've trained a good few circus dogs in my time! He loved his job, and nothing else, as for the rest, he was a duffer. Towards the end you wouldn't have given a bob for him had you seen him by day, he looked so old, fourteen he must have been, at least, and that stiff from the rheumatics, with his eyes running and his black muzzle going all grey. He only began to wake up when the time for his act came round;

it was then that he was well worth seeing! I used to doll him up like a movie star, with black cosmetic on his nose, thick pencil round his poor old rheumy eyes, I'd starch-powder him all over to make him white as snow, then add the blue ribbons! My word, Madame, he soon came alive again! Hardly had I finished his make-up, when off he went, walking on his hind legs, sneezing, and carrying on no end till the curtain rose. Back in the wings again, I used to wrap him in a blanket and then give him a spirit rub. I certainly prolonged his life, but no performing poodle can last for ever!

"My two bitches there, they do their work all right, but it's not the same thing at all. They love their master, they fear the whip, they use their heads and are conscientious, but there's no professional pride in their make up. They go through their routine as though they were pulling a cart, no more, no less. They're hard workers, but they're not true artistes. It's easy to see from their faces that they'd like to be through with the whole performance, and the public don't like that. Either they think the animals are playing them up, or else they make no bones about saying 'Poor beasts, how sad they look! What tortures they must have endured to learn all those monkey tricks!' I'd just like to watch 'em, all those ladies and gentlemen of the 'Protection for Animals', trying to put the dogs through their paces. Why, they'd do exactly like me and my sort. Sugar, hunting-crop; hunting-crop, sugar; with a good dose of patience added: there's no other way that I know of."

At this very moment the "hard workers" are eyeing each other with hostile intent. Manette, perched on a block of multicoloured wood, is nervously trembling; while, facing her, Cora has laid her ears back flat like a sorry cat.

At the shrill of the bell, the orchestra interrupts the heavy polka, intended to calm the public's impatience, with the opening bars of a slow valse; as if obeying a signal, the two dogs adjust their position: they have recognised *their* valse. Cora gently swishes her tail, pricks her ears, and takes on the neutral expression, amiable and bored, which makes her resemble the portraits of Empress Eugénie. Manette, insolent, alert, rather too fat, awaits the painfully slow rise of the curtain and Harry's arrival on the scene, yawns, and starts panting at once, from exasperation and thirst.

The act begins, without incident, without rebellion. Cora, forewarned by a flick of the whip under her belly, does not cheat while taking her jumps. Manette walks on her front legs, valses, barks, and jumps a few obstacles erect on the back of the yellow collie. Their performance is commonplace, but correct; there is nothing to be said against it.

Inveterate grumblers may find fault, perhaps, with Cora's queenly aloofness, or with the small terrier's artificial zest. It's easy to see that such grouchers have not got months of touring in their paws, and know nothing of the horrors of guard's vans, hostels, bread-and-meat mash that distends but does not nourish, the long hours of waiting in railway stations, the too short constitutional walks, the iron collar, the muzzle, and above all the eternal waiting, the nerve-racking wait for exercise, for starting out, for food, for a thrashing. These exacting spectators ignore the fact that the life of performing animals is spent in waiting, and that this wears them out.

Tonight both dogs are waiting for nothing but the end of their turn. No sooner is the curtain down, than a pitched battle ensues. Harry returns to the scene just in time to part the pair of them, flecked with pink nips, their ribbons in tatters.

"It's something quite new for them, Madame, something they've picked up while they've been here," he cries in a fury. "As a rule they're very good friends, they sleep together in my hotel bedroom. But here, why it's only a small town, you see. You can't pick and choose here. The inn-keeper's wife said to me 'I'll put up with one dog, but I'll not take two!' So, as I like to deal fair, I let first one, then the other of my two bitches spend the night in the theatre, in a padlocked basket. They cottoned on to the rotation right away. And now, every night, they go through the high jinks you've just witnessed. All through the day they're as meek as lambs; as the hour approaches to buckle one in, it's a fight to decide which won't be the one to stay behind in the locked basket; they'd tear each other to shreds, they're so jealous! And you've not seen the half of it! It's a proper show to watch the performance of the one I'm taking back with me, when she starts yapping her head off and scampering round the basket as I shut the lid on the other! I don't like to be unfair to animals, not me! I'd do anything rather than what I have to do here, but since there is nothing else for it, how can I?"

I did not see Manette tonight, as she took her leave, arrogant and radiating joy; but I did see the imprisoned Cora, rigid with repressed despair. Her lovely golden fleece was crumpled against the wicker sides of the basket, and through the bars at the top poked out her long, gentle, fox-like nose.

She listened to the receding sounds of her master's footsteps and Manette's tinkling bell. When the iron door finally closed behind then, she drew in a long breath to let out a howl; but she remembered that I was still there, and all I heard was a deep human sigh. Then she proudly closed her eyes and settled down for the night.

THE CHILD PRODIGY

"Really, there are a great many children in this show, I find; do you not agree, Madame?"

This remark is flung at me, in supercilious and superior tones, by a large blonde lady—*Spécialité, Valses lentes*—who for the moment is bundled in a crepon kimono costing seven francs fifty, the sort of kimono invariably found in all music-hall dressing-rooms. Hers is pink, with storks printed on it; mine is blue, sprinkled with small red and green fans, and that of the dove-trainer is mauve, with black flowers.

The stout, discontented lady has just been jostled by three kids no taller than fox hounds, dressed as Red Indians, who were rushing off to remove their make-up. But her bitter words were directed at a silent creature, a sort of unhappy governess dressed all in black, slowly pacing up and down the corridor.

Having spoken, the stout lady gives a slight cough, in a most distinguished manner, and retires to her dressing-room, but not before throwing a last contemptuous glance at the governess, who shrugs her shoulders and smiles vaguely at me.

"She intended that remark for me. She finds there are too many children in the show! Very well, what about me in that case, I'm to start by removing my own child, I suppose!"

"What, you can't mean that you're dissatisfied? 'Princess Lily' is surely a success?"

"Yes, and don't I know it! My daughter is quite devastating, isn't she? Yes, she's my daughter, my real daughter. . . . Wait a second and I'll button you up at the back, you can't possibly manage it yourself! Besides, I'm in no hurry, myself. My daughter's gone to the hairdresser to have her ringlets set. I'd so much like to stay with you for a while. All the more, on account of her and me having had words just now."

In the mirror behind me I can see a plain humble face with moist eyes.

"She certainly answered me back just now! I tell you, Madame, that child fair takes me to pieces, for all that she's only thirteen. Oh, she don't look her age, I know, but then she's dressed to look so much younger on the stage. I'm not telling you all this to deny her, or to say anything against her."

"No flattery intended, but I'd be the first to agree that nothing could look sweeter or prettier than she does when she plays her piece on the violin in that white baby frock of hers. Or when she sings her Italian song—you've seen her, have you, in that little Neapolitan boy's costume? And her American dance, have you seen that too?

"The public can soon tell the difference between a dainty number like my girl's and one like those three little miseries who've just gone rushing off. They're so scraggy, Madame, and they look so scared, too. Those frightened eyes they roll at the smallest mistake they make in their work! As I was saying only the other day to my Lily, 'They make a pitiful sight!' 'Phoui!' she gives me for answer, 'they're not interesting.' I know well enough it's that competitive spirit in her that makes her say things like that, but all the same she comes out with remarks that knock the stuffing out of me.

"I'm telling you all this, but you'll keep it to yourself,

you won't let it go any further, will you? I feel a bit
nervy today because she's answered me back just now,
me, her mother!

"Oh, I can't say I bless the man who put Lily on the
stage! Fine gentleman though he is, and a good writer
of plays. I used to work for his lady, by the day, embroid-
ering fine linen. His lady was very kind to me, and
allowed Lily to come and wait for me there when she
came out of school.

"One day, it must be nearly four years since, the gentleman I was speaking of was on the look-out for a clever
child to take a little girl's part in one of his plays, and for
a lark he asked me for my Lily. . . . It was soon settled,
Madame. My little girl had them all flabbergasted from
the start. Poise, memory, proper intonation, she'd got all
that and more. I didn't take it too serious at first till I
heard they'd pay Lily up to eight francs a day. There
was nothing you could say against that, was there?

"After that play came another, and then another. And
every time I'd say 'After success like that, it's the last
time Lily will act.' They all got after me. 'Now stop all
this nonsense! Just drop that damned embroidery job of
yours! Can't you see you've got a gold mine in that
child! Not to mention you've no right to stifle a talent
like hers.' And so on and so forth, till I hardly dared
breathe. . . .

"And during that time, you should have seen the progress my little one made! Hobnobbing with the celebri-
ties, and saying 'My dear' to the manager himself! And
grave as a judge with it all, which made everyone split
their sides.

"Then came the time, two years ago, when my
daughter found herself out of a job. 'Thank the Lord,'
I says to myself, 'now we can have a rest, and settle down

on the nice little sum we've put by from the theatre.' I consult Lily, as was my duty; she'd already made a big impression on me with her knowing ways. Can you guess what she answered? 'My poor Mama, you must be crackers! I shan't always be eleven, unfortunately. This is not the time to go to sleep. There's nothing doing in the theatre this season, but the music-hall's there all right, for me to have a go!'

"As you may imagine, Madame, she didn't lack encouragement from these, and those, and especially the others, none of whose business it was! Gifted as she is, it didn't take her long to learn to dance and sing. Her chief worry is that she's growing up. I have to measure her every fortnight: she'd like so much to stay small! Only last month she flew into a rage because she'd put on two centimetres in the last year, and reproached me for not having made her a dwarf from birth.

"It's terrible, the manner of speaking she's picked up back stage, and her bossiness, too! She soon gets the upper hand, I being so weak. She argued back at me again today. She'd been that lah-di-dah in her answers, that for a moment I saw red and got on my high horse. 'And so what! I'm your mother, I'd have you know! And supposing I took you by the arm and put a stop to you going on with the theatre!'

"She was busy making up her eyes; she didn't even turn round, she just started to laugh. 'Stop me going on with the theatre? Ha! Ha! Ha! And I suppose you'd go on in my place and sing them *Chiribibibi* to pay the rent!'

"Tears came to my eyes, Madame: it's hard when one is humiliated by one's own flesh and blood. But it's not altogether that I feel so bad about. It's . . . I'm not sure how to explain what it is. There are times when I look at her and think 'She's my little daughter, and she's thirteen.

She's been four years in show business. Rehearsals, back-stage tittle-tattle, unfair treatment on the part of the manager, rivalry between the stars, jealousy of her comrades, her posters, the band-leader who bears her a grudge, the call-boy who was too late—or too soon—with her bell, the claque, her costume-maker. . . . That's all she's had in her head and on her lips for the last four years. All these past four years I've never once heard her talk like a child. . . . And never, never, never again shall I hear her talk like a child—like a real child. . . ."

THE MISFIT

I

THE stagehands called her "a choice piece"; but the Schmetz family—eight acrobats, their mother, wives, and "young ladies"—never mentioned her; Ida and Hector, "Duo Dancers", said severely "she brings shame on the house". Jady, the "*diseuse*" from Montmartre, made use of her most rasping contralto to exclaim, on seeing her, "Well, what d'you know about that number!" and was quizzed in reply with imperious disdain, and the flashy deployment of a long ermine stole.

For the public this outcast was billed as "La Roussalka"; but for the entire caf'-conc' personnel she became, on the spot, "Poison Ivy". Within the span of a mere six days the austere back-stage staff of the Élysée-Pigalle were at their wits' end, and deplored her superfluous presence. Dancer? Singer? Pah! Neither the one, nor t'other. . . .

"She displaces air, that's all!" Brague assured everyone.

She sang Russian songs and danced the *jota*, the *sevillana* and the *tango*, revised and corrected by an Italian ballet-master—Spanish, ollé! with a Frenchified flavour!

No sooner was Friday's band-call over, than the whole house was eyeing her askance. La Roussalka chose to rehearse in a carefully considered liberty gown and hat, hands in muff, indicating the *jota* with discreet little jerks of her hobble-skirted posterior, stopping abruptly to shout "That's not it, Jesus! That's not it!", stamping and screaming "Brutes!" at the members of the band.

Mutter Schmetz, who sat mending her sons' tights in the circle, could hardly be kept in her seat. "That, an *ardisde!* That, a *tanzer!* Ach! she is nozzings but a *dard,* yes?"

And La Roussalka continued, "with enough brazen cheek to gobble up her parents", to employ Brague's energetic metaphor, bullying the property man, cursing the electrician, demanding a blue flood on her entrance, and a red spot on her exit, and goodness knows what else!

"I've played all the big houses in Europe," she yelled, "and I've neverrr seen a joint so disgrrracefully rrrun!"

She rolled her 'r's' in a most insulting manner, as if she were chucking a handful of pebbles straight in your face.

During this rehearsal one saw nothing but La Roussalka, and heard nothing but La Roussalka. In the evening, however, it was discovered that there were two of them: opposite La Roussalka, dark, ablaze with purple spangles and imitation topazes, danced a soft, fair-haired child, graceful, light as air. "This is my sisterrr," La Roussalka declared, though no one had asked for enlightenment. Further, she had an offensive way of clinching matters, on her "worrrd of honourrr", that shocked even her most candid listener.

Whether sister, servile poor relation, or a little dancer hired for a pittance—nobody knew or cared. She appeared, a mere chit of a girl, to be dancing in her sleep, docile as a lamb, pretty, with huge, vacant, brown eyes. At the end of the *sevillana,* she rested a moment against a flat, mouth agape, then noiselessly returned to the cellar, while La Roussalka started on her *tango.*

"What's more," Brague said for all to hear, "she dances with her hands!"

Hands, arms, hips, eyes, eyebrows, hair—her feet, being unskilled, did not know what they were up to. What saved the day for her was the cocksure flamboyance, the assured insolence of her least gesture. She congratulated herself if she made a false step, seemed highly delighted if she fluffed an entrechat and, back in the wings, gave herself no time to draw breath before starting to talk, talk, talk, and lie with all the abandon of a Southerner born in Russia.

She addressed herself to the world in general with the familiarity of a tipsy princess. She stopped one of the blond Schmetz boys, in his pale mauve tights, by laying both hands on his shoulders, so that with lowered eyes and blushing, he dared not make good his escape; she forcibly drove Mutter Schmetz into a corner, only to be met with a volley of *Ja, Ja, Ja*s as stinging as smacks in the face; the facetious stage-manager got more than he bargained for in the way of abuse, as did Brague, who kept whistling throughout her tirade.

"My family. . . . My native land. . . . I'm a Russian. . . . I speak fourteen languages, like all my compatriots. . . . I've gotten myself six thousand francs worth of stage-costumes for this wretched little number worth nothing at all. . . . But you should see, my dearrr, all the town clothes I have! Money means nothing to me! . . . I can't tell you my real name: there's no knowing what might happen if I did! My father holds the most important position in Moscow. He's married, you know. Only he's not married to my mother. . . . He gives me everything I want. . . . You've seen my sister? She's a good-for-nothing. I beat her a lot, she won't work. All I can say is she's pure! On my life, she's that! . . . You none of you saw me last year in Berlin? Oh, that's where you should have seen me! A thirty-two-thousand-franc act, my dearrr! With that blackguard Castillo, the dancer. He robbed me, on my worrrd of honourr, he stole from me! But once across the Russian border and I told my father everything. Castillo was jugged! In Russia, we show no mercy to thieves. Jugged, I tell you, jugged! Like this!"

She went through the motions of turning a key in its lock, and her heavily violet-pencilled eyes sparkled with cruelty. Then, played out, she went down to her dressing-room where she relieved her nervous tension by giving her "sister" more than one good clout on the ears. Genuine stage slaps they were, resounding right enough, but they rang true on those young cheeks. They could be heard up on the stage. Mutter Schmetz, outraged, spoke of "gomblaining to de bolice" and pressed to her bosom two flaxen-haired lads of seven and eight, the youngest born of her flaxen-haired brood, as if "Poison Ivy" were about to give them a spanking.

By what noxious flames was this fiend of a woman consumed? Before the week was out, she had hurled a satin slipper at the band-leader's head, referred to the secretary-general, in his hearing, as a "pimp" and, by accusing her dresser of stealing her jewellery, reduced the poor creature to tears. Gone were the quiet evenings of the Élysée-Pigalle and the peaceful slumbers of its cells behind closed doors! Gone for good! "Poison Ivy" had ruined everything.

"She's out for my blood, is she!" was Jady's bold threat. "Let me hear one single word from that one, no, not even that, let her so much as brush against me in the doorway, and I'll get her fired!"

Brague, for once, might well have supported Jady, for

he could not stomach the unwarrantable success of La Roussalka, and the way she glittered among the mended tights, home-cleaned dresses, and smoke-blackened scenery, like a sham jewel in an imitation setting.

"I enjoy my rest," Ida whispered to Brague. "There's never been so much as a word uttered against my husband and me, you know that! Well then, I can assure you, that *when* I leave the stage, you know, *when* I carry Hector off standing on my hands, and I catch sight of 'Poison Ivy' sniggering at the two of us, it wouldn't need much for me to drop Hector plonk on her head!"

Nobody bothered any more about the little blonde "sister", who never uttered a word and danced like a sleep-walker between one stinging blow and the next. She was to be met with in the corridors, her shoulder weighed down by a slop-pail or a pitcher full of water, shuffling along in bedraggled old slippers, her petticoats trailing behind her.

But after the show, La Roussalka rigged her out in a loosely belted dress, too voluminous for her flat-chested figure, and a hat that came half way down her back, and whisked her off, red-cheeked from her drubbing and gummy-eyed, to the night-haunts on the Butte de Montmartre. There she made her sit down, docile and half-asleep, with cocktails in front of her, and once again, to the cynical amazement of chance "friends", she started to talk and talk and tell lies.

"My father . . . the most influential man in Moscow. . . . I speak fourteen languages. . . . I myself never tell lies; but my compatriots, the Russians, are one and all liars. . . . I've sailed twice round the world on a princely yacht. . . . My jewels are all in Moscow, for my family forbids me to wear them on the stage, because of the ducal coronets on every piece. . . ."

Meanwhile the little sister dozed on half-awake. From time to time she almost took a somersault when one of the "friends" tried to squeeze her thin waist or stroke her bare neck, pale mauve with pearl powder. Her surprise unloosed the rage of La Roussalka.

"Wake up, you, where do you think you are? Jesus! what a life, having to drag this child around with me!"

Calling to witness not only the "friends", but the restaurant at large, she shouted "Look at her there, that good-for-nothing! This table couldn't hold the piles of dough I've spent on her! I'm reduced to tears the whole day long because she will do nothing, nothing, nothing!"

The slapped child never batted an eyelid. Of what youthful past, or of what escape, was she dreaming behind her mysteriously vacant, huge brown eyes?

II

"This child," Brague decrees, "is a kid we'll stick in the chorus. One more, one less, it makes little difference. She'll always earn her forty sous . . . though I don't much like having to deal with misfits. . . . I say this now so's it's known another time."

Brague speaks pontifically, in his dark kingdom of the Élysée-Pigalle, where his double function of mime and producer assure him undisputed authority.

The "misfit", or so it would seem, pays no heed to his words. Her vague thanks are expressed in a meaningless smile that does not spread to her large eyes, the colour of clouded coffee, and she lingers on, arms limp, twiddling the handle of a faded bag.

She has just this moment been christened by Brague: henceforth she will be known as "Misfit". A week ago she was the "good-for-nothing little sister"; she gains by the change.

Little matter, for she discourages malice, and even attention, this foundling who has just been dumped down here, without a sound, by "La Roussalka, her sister", who went off leaving her with three torn silk under-slips, a couple of "latest models" sizes too big for her, a pair of evening shoes with Strass paste buckles, not to mention a hat, and the key to the room they occupied together in the Rue Fontaine.

La Roussalka, *alias* "Poison Ivy", that human hurricane, that storm-cloud charged with hail ready to burst at the least shock, has shown in her flight a strange discretion, by removing her four large trunks, her "family papers", the portrait of her *fatherrr* "who controls rain and sunshine in Moscow", while forgetting the little sister who danced with her, docile, half asleep, and somehow weighed down by blows.

"Misfit" neither wept nor wailed. She stated her case to the lady manager in a few words and with a Flemish accent exactly suited to her blonde sheep-like appearance. Madame did not overflow with maternal protestations or pitying indignation, any more than did Jady, the *diseuse*, or Brague himself. "Misfit" has attained the age of eighteen, and is therefore old enough to go out alone and look after her own affairs.

"Eighteen!" Jady grumbled, suffering from a hangover and bronchitis. "Eighteen, and she expects me to take pity on her!"

Brague, a good fellow at heart, felt more kindly disposed. "Forty sous, did I say? We'll bloody well give three francs, so's to give her time to look round."

Since then "Misfit" comes every day, at one, to sit in one of the canvas-covered stalls of the Élysée-Pigalle, and wait. When Brague calls out "On stage, the great hetairae!", she climbs on to the gangway that spans the orchestra pit and sits down at a sticky zinc table such as is used in low pubs. In the pantomime now in rehearsal she will take the part, wearing a reconditioned pink gown, of an "elegant customer" at a Montmartre cabaret.

She can hardly be seen from the auditorium, since she has been placed at the very back of the stage, behind the huge, seedy-looking hats of the other ladies of the chorus. The stage-hand sets in front of her an empty glass and a spoon, and there she poses, her childish chin resting on a dubiously gloved hand.

She is a thoroughly safe customer. She doesn't jabber on the stage, never complains of the icy draught whistling round her legs, nor has she either the unhappy look of young Miriam, so furiously hungry that it seems to demand food, or Vanda's feverish activity, Vanda the Cluck, for ever producing from her pocket a baby's sock in need of darning, or a flannelette brassière that she mends while trying to hide it.

"Misfit" has fallen into oblivion again, apparently thankful at last to be able to roll up into a ball, as though the general indifference has spared her the trouble of existing. She speaks even less than the star dancer from Milan, a heavy woman, pitted with smallpox and plastered with holy medals and coral callosities. Her silence, at any rate, is born of contempt, she being interested solely in the "five points", the *entrechats-six*, the whole graceless and laborious range of acrobatics that exercise the sailor's muscles on her calves.

Up stage, Brague is doing his level best not to husband an ounce of his energy. "Isn't he lucky to sweat like that!" sighs the wretched brat Miriam, white with cold under her rouge. Brague sweats in vain at his miming. He wears himself out trying to communicate his faith, his feverish enthusiasm, to the little tart in her hairless fur, to the stubborn mender of baby socks, to the arrogant ballerina. He insists—oh, the folly of it!—that Miriam, Wanda, and the Italian should at least appear to take an interest in the action of his piece.

"I'm telling you . . . Good God! I'm trying to tell you this is the moment when these two characters are starting to fight! When two chaps start a fight close beside you, doesn't it effect you more than that? Good God, do stir your stumps! At least say Ah! as you would when there's a brawl in a pub and you pick up your skirts ready to fly!"

After the sound and the fury of an hour's effort, Brague takes a rest, finding some compensation in running through his big scene, the scene where he reads the letter from his mother. Joy and surprise, then terror, and finally despair, are depicted on features seamed with such intensity of expression, such excess of pathos, that Wanda stops sewing, Miriam slapping the soles of her feet, and the Italian dancer, swathed in a grey woollen shawl, deigns to leave the framework of a flat to watch Brague's tears flow. A minor daily triumph, delectable all the same.

On each such an occasion, however, a faint chortle like a smothered laugh has spoilt this affecting moment. Brague's sharp ear caught it from the very first day.

The second day: "Which of you ladies is the chuckle-head that's convulsed with laughter?" he shouts. No answer, and the dismal faces of the "great hetairae" reveal nothing.

The third day: "There's a fine of forty sous about to fall on somebody's nut—and I know very well who it is— for causing a disturbance during rehearsal!" But Brague does not know who it is.

The fourth day: "You there, Misfit, are you trying to get a rise out of me?" Brague storms. "You wear yourself to a shadow, yes, you strive to put into what you're doing a little . . . of the tragic side of life, of . . . simple truth and beauty, you try to pull the mimodrama out of the common rut, only to succeed in what? In reducing misfits like you to a state of hopeless giggles!"

A chair falls, and the pale trembling form of Misfit rises from out of the Stygian gloom, bleating like a goat. "But Mon . . . Monsieur Brague, I . . . I'm not laughing, I'm crying!"

III

I'm really a wonderful guy,
So fond of the kiddies am I,
The nice sweet little dears . . .
Garn, the little perishers!

"Misfit" leans against an iron strut, swaying like a small chained bear as she automatically rubs her powdered shoulder-blades to and fro against the cold metal. She listens, while gazing from a distance at the character whom the Compère is about to introduce to the Commère as a choice tit-bit, by gently pressing forefinger to thumb as if he held between them a folded butterfly.

"Plebiscites are all the fashion, my dear friend: I am happy to present to you tonight the man who, by an impressive majority, has been newly elected the Prince of Mirth—our joyous friend, adventurer and companion —Sarracq!"

'The frock-coat don't fit him half as well as Raffort,' thinks Misfit. 'And you could see even then it hadn't been made to fit Raffort.'

She notes the difference between the pearl-grey frock-coat that hangs too long and loose on Sarracq and the violet silk tail-coat that trusses the stout body of the Compere, who does his best, by rounding his arms and shoulders, to conceal the shortness of his sleeves. As he steps up on to the stage again, his back to the public, he turns sideways and draws in his waist, to ease the tightness of the knee-breeches that are squeezing the life out of him.

An ominous heat hangs heavy on the close of the evening performance. The exasperation is due not so much to the storm that is about to break into a torrential downpour, as to the fact that it is one more August night in a succession of cloudless days and nights without a drop of rain. It is a merciless summer heat that has slowly penetrated through the dim recesses of the wings down to the musty lower regions of the Empyrée-Palace. The performers know it well. Shouts of laughter are no longer heard; even the chorus-girls' dressing-rooms, wide open to the corridors, no longer resound with the tumult of envigorating slanging-matches. From the Commere to the grips and flymen, all creep about cautiously, with the economy of movement of shipwrecked people determined to harbour the last ounce of their strength.

"Matinée tomorrow!" thinks "Misfit". She droops her head like a cab-horse and, without seeing them, gazes down at her satin shoes already agape where the big toes poke through. She is revived by the refreshing whiff of ether and smelling salts. 'Yes, of course, for Elsie, who's a bit off colour. She's struck lucky, as you might say! She's through with it for the evening!"

Four skinny little creatures, in embroidered linen frocks, put in an appearance one after the other on the iron stairs. Their silent passage seems to attract "Misfit" like a magnet, and she follows them as if sleep-walking. With the same uncertain step, they file on to the stage one after the other, sing an indistinct little ditty about the games little girls get up to, at the same time kicking up their legs and baby-frock skirts, and then return breathless to the wings.

When "Misfit", leaning against her iron stay, exhales an almost inaudible, desperate "Oh, this heat!", one of the four *Babies* breaks into a nervous laugh, as if "Misfit" had said something terribly funny.

The Summer Revue, condemned to survive until the first of September, is in the throes of its last agony. It plays to pitiful second houses where some two hundred spectators, dispersed over the echoing auditorium, eye one another with embarrassment and disappear before the Grand Finale. It comes to life again on certain Saturdays, or a rainy Sunday, when the galleries are crammed with a malodorous crowd.

With prudence verging on the cynical, the management has removed one by one from the cast all the expensive stars of the original production. The English male dancer turned up his nose at the Parisian summer; the operetta star now gives Trouville the benefit of her soprano; a hundred performances have exhausted relays of Commeres. Sarracq, idol of the Left Bank, has stepped into the frock-coat of Raffort, who himself had succeeded the English dancer, and thus elevated to top of the bill a name quite honestly unknown on this side of the bridges.

Only the costumes have not been renewed, the costumes and "Misfit". Ever since the day when her temperamental sister, the *danseuse*, deposited her on the theatre doorstep three years since, "Misfit" has been part of the house, appearing in the chorus of all the Revues, Panto-mimes and Ballets. Luck had it one day that the man-ager took notice of her to the extent of enquiring "And what's that little girl over there?"

"She's one of the three francs thirty-threes," the stage-manager replied.

As from the day following a dazzled "Misfit" had her salary raised from a hundred to a hundred and sixty francs a month. This change entailed putting in an appear-ance for endless hours spent in bovine rumination, or in work more stultifying than abject idleness—parades, chorus routine, or plastic poses. Summer and winter alike come and go without releasing her, and her soft young eyelids are already swollen by fatigue into two lymphatic pouches. She is sweet and gentle, with large submissive eyes, so much so that the stage-manager refers to her by turns as "the cream of the regulars," or "the dumb-bell of the duds".

Tonight she is feeling the heat like the rest of the world, and even more than the others because she has eaten next to nothing. The mere thought of her dinner makes her feel sick; she imagines she is still sitting at an outside table with an untouched plate of hot beef going cold in front of her. There are also the green peas that smell of wet dog. She shakes the curls of her thick wig against her cheeks and slowly starts towards the iron stairs. She is in no haste to quit the spot where she is slowly, peacefully, fading away in a sort of funereal security. Before going down below, she risks a peep through the curtain slit and murmurs apprehensively, "Oh, it's packed full of savages again tonight!"

The fact is "Misfit" is afraid of summer audiences. She knows that the regular quiet shop-keepers who frequent the Empyrée-Place reliquish their seats in August to strange hordes of foreigners whose raucous hubbub during the intervals she finds disquieting. She has an equal horror of rough teutonic beards, oriental hard blue-black hair-pads and oily skins, and impenetrable negro smiles. . . . It must be the heat that brings them, with all the other scourges of these dog-days.

"Misfit" is not ignorant of the fact that "savages", in the deserted streets after midnight, follow and solicit pale and anaemic little chorus girls, whose theatre salary is three francs thirty-three a day.

"One's got to live, of course," thinks "Misfit", with her sorry nag's resignation. "But not with these, not with those, not those *savages*!"

She has quite made up her mind to go home alone, come what may. However worn out she may be, she will walk as far as Caulaincourt on the other side of the bridge. There her scorching small room awaits her, at the very top of a boarding-house overlooking the Montmartre cemetery. The thin walls keep the heat all night long and what wind there is brings factory smoke only.

It is not a room to live in, let alone to sleep in. But "Misfit" has bought a half pound of plums, and these she will eat all alone, in her chemise, beside the window. . . . This is her one summer luxury. She plays the game of squeezing the stones between finger and thumb and then seeing how far she can shoot them, even as far as the cemetery. When, in the silence before dawn, she hears a stone rebound from an iron crucifix and strike with a musical ring a glass pane of the chapel, she smiles as she says to herself "I've won!"

FROM THE FRONT

"LA FENICE"

"WHAT is there to do tonight?"

Drenched throughout the day, Naples has been steaming like a dirty bath. The bay lies flattened by the continual rain, and Capri has melted away behind the rigid silvery downpour. A spectacular curtain of bluish-purple cloud veils and unveils Vesuvius from view and trails on down as far as the sea, where it finally shrouds the sky, crushing, as the sun sets, the living red rose that lay half open in its midst.

The tinkle of a bell echoes through the empty white hotel where we brave cholera and hail squalls. We could run or bowl a hoop down the interminable corridor under the dreary eye of the German waiters. We have the billiard-room to ourselves and the bar—where the man in the white waistcoat is asleep—all the lifts and the crinkly-haired chambermaids with lovely eyes and fat shiny noses. We own the dining-room—with places laid for two hundred guests—isolated from us by a three-fold screen that prevents our seeing the half-acre of polished parquet floor, dazzlingly bright . . . but . . .

"What is there to do tonight?"

In the first place, consult the barometer. Then, forehead pressed against the french window of the verandah, gaze out over the flooded quayside to watch, swaying in its iron gibbet, the electric globe big as a mauve moon as it swings in the wind.

Between one gusty squall and the next, a voice sings *Bella mia* and *Fa me dormi*: a child's voice, shrill, metallic, nasal, sustained by mandolines. All of a sudden I am startled to see, on the other side of the window pane, a forehead pressed against mine, two eyes trying to look into my eyes, a pair of dark eyes under the weather-beaten disorder of picturesque hair: the young girl who was singing has come up the terrace steps in search of her half lira. I open the door a little way; the child has barely slipped in before she makes good her escape, after a confidingly suppliant gesture, a quick, utterly feminine, almost blush-making glance of appraisal. She glistens with rain-drops under her stiff mantle with its pointed hood; a smell of ponds and soaking wet wool has come in with her.

"What is there to do tonight? Tell me, say something, what can we do tonight?"

Half an hour later we find ourselves stranded at "*La Fenice*", a caf'-conc' of moderate size, plastered all over—walls, drop-curtain, passages—with posters glorifying a local liqueur in a riot of publicity. Insipid in design, the outmoded silhouettes of the women displayed, high-bosomed and high-waisted, suffice to make us feel suddenly very far from Paris, and a little lost.

Despite two glaring flood-lights, the place as a whole remains dismal; there are exactly three women in the audience, two little countrified, shabbily dressed tarts and myself. But the men are there in their hordes! While waiting for the curtain to rise they laugh uproariously, hum to the rhythm of the band, shake hands with one another, and bandy quips across the house;

here reigns the familiarity found in places of ill repute.

But, on the programme, what a regiment of women! And what lovely Italian names, Gemma la Bellissima, Lorenza, Lina, Maria! Among this bevy I madly hope for red-haired Venetian beauties with pink-and-white skins, Roman goddesses pale under raven black hair, Florentines with aristocratic chins. . . . Alas! . . .

Against a crudely painted blackcloth, on which I certainly never expected this scene of a French château mirrored in the Loire, file past Lina, Maria, Lorenza, and Gemma la Bellissima, and countless others. The frailest of them humiliates the caryatids that support the balcony. Here, the solid is patently preferred. So much so that I suspect Lorenza di Gloria of having supplied, with considerable aid from cotton wadding and rolled-up handkerchiefs, a suitable substitute for what is lacking in the still angular body of a young Jewess; for she waves a pair of skinny arms, yellow under the armpits, round and about an enormous bust and all along inflated hips draped in woven satin, violet and gold.

A shattering storm of applause greets—but why?—Gemma la Bellissima, a flaccid dancing-girl in green gauze. She is "the Dancer in the Nude", whose bashful antics are noisily acclaimed and accompanied, while her reserved smile acts as an apology for having to display so much! At one moment, turning her too white back to the audience, she goes so far as to attempt a lascivious wriggle; but she quickly turns round again, as though wounded by the glances, to resume, eyes suitably lowered, her little game as a modest washerwoman, wringing and shaking out her spangled veil.

The local star performer is worth listening to, and looking at as well. She is Maria X, an Italian approaching her fifties, still beautiful, and cleverly pargeted. I cannot deny, nor do I reject, the appeal of her well-trained voice, already going, and of her over-demonstrative gestures. Nor will I dispute that she possesses a natural instinct for mime which enables her to "convey the meaning" with face, shoulders, curve of the waist, plump yet responsive legs, but above all with her hands; indefatigable hands that mould, weigh, and caressingly stroke the empty air, while her weary features, bright, seductive, express laughter or tears, or become creased with wrinkles regardless of the cracks they create in her heavy make-up, till with a single knife-edged glance, with a contraction of her proud velvety eyebrows, she compels the lustful attention of the entire audience.

"Lucette de Nice." . . . I have been looking forward to the appearance of the little French girl who bears such a pretty, childish name. Here she is. Slimness personified— at last! Rather misery-stricken in her short and heavily spangled dress, she sings hackneyed Parisian ditties. Where have I seen this slovenly yet graceful errand-girl before, with no nose to speak of, and a sulky look as though she were afraid? At Olympia, perhaps? Or at the Gaîté-Rochechouart?

Lucette de Nice. . . . She knows but one gesture, a curious scooping movement of the hand, not unlike a cat, preposterous but somehow pleasing. Where have I seen her? Her roving eyes encounter mine, and her smile leaves her lips to be transferred to her large blue-pencilled eyes. She has recognised me too, and never again takes her eyes off me. She gives no further thought to her words. I can read on her poor-little-girl features the longing to join me, to talk to me. When she comes to the end of her song she gives me a fleeting smile, like someone about to cry, then hurriedly leaves the stage, knocking her arm against the entrance.

After that, there is yet another heavy, healthy girl, full of confidence but not fully awake, who scatters among the audience stalkless flowers attached to light pliable reeds. She is followed by a female acrobat, undisguisedly pregnant, who appears to find her act a torture and takes her bow with a distraught look on a face beaded with sweat.

Too many women, oh, far too many women! I could wish this flock enlivened by some fruity Neapolitan comic or the inevitable tenor with blue hair. Five or six poodles would not spoil the show, nor would a *cornet-à-piston* player who tries out his skill on a box of cigars.

Such a welter of females becomes depressing! One sees them at too close range, one's thoughts go out to them. My eyes wander from the threadbare false hem to the tarnished gilt of a girdle, from the dim little ring to the pink-dipped white coral necklace. And then my eye lights on the red wrists under a coat of wet white, on hands hardened by cooking, washing, and sweeping; I surmise the laddered stockings and the leaf-thin soles; I imagine the grimy stairs leading up to the fireless room and the short-lived light of the candle. . . . While gazing up at the present singer, I see the others, all the others. . . .

"What do you say to our leaving?"

The deluge continues. A raging gale drives the downpour under the raised hood of our carriage as we go bouncing away, drawn by a devil-possessed crazy small black nag, that seems hell-bent under the encouragement of the frenzied bellowings of a hump-backed cabby.

"GITANETTE"

Ten o'clock. There has been so much smoking in the Semiramis Bar tonight that my compote of apples has a vague flavour of Virginian cigarettes. . . . It is Saturday night. A kind of holiday-fever exists among the regulars in anticipation of the rest-day tomorrow, that exceptional day so unlike all the others, with the long lie in bed in the morning, the drive-out in a taxi-cab as far as the Pavillon-Bleu, the visit to relations, the outing for the kids shut up in some suburban boarding-school who will be coming, on this lovely Sunday morning, to have a breath of the fresh envigorating air of Le Châtelet.

Semiramis herself is up to her eyes in work, and has already put on a monster stock-pot to serve as the main basis for her Sunday dinners. "Thirty pounds of beef, my dear, and the giblets of half a dozen chicken! That should keep them going for some time, I'm thinking, and allow me a few moments' peace, for I'll be able to serve it first as the main course for dinner, and then cold with salad for supper. And as for soup, just think of all the soup they'll be able to have!" She is by now much calmer, smoking her everlasting cigarette as she parades from table to table her good ogress smile and her whisky-and-soda, from which unthinkingly she takes an occasional sip. The strong bitter coffee is getting cold in my cup; my bitch, her nose running from the cigarette smoke, urges me to leave.

"You don't recognise me?" says a voice close beside me.

A young woman, simply, almost poorly clad in black, is looking at me with enquiring eyes. It is hard to tell the true colour of her hair under her matted-straw hat trimmed with quills; she is wearing a white collar with a neat tie, and her pearl-grey gloves are slightly soiled.

Her face is powdered, her lips are rouged, her eye-lashes darkened with mascara: the indispensable make-up, but applied without due consideration, of necessity, from force of habit. I ransack my memory, when suddenly the lovely eyes, with huge pupils the shimmering dark brown of Semiramis' coffee, bring me the answer.

"Why, of course, you're Gitanette!"

Her name, her absurd music-hall name, has come back to me, and with it the memory of where we met.

It must have been three or four years ago, at the time I was playing in the Empyrée Pantomime, that Gitanette occupied the dressing-room next to mine. Gitanette and her girl-friend, "A Duo in Cosmopolitan Dances", used to dress with their door open on to the passage to get more air. Gitanette took the male parts and her girl-friend—Rita, Lina, Nina?—appeared, turn by turn, as a drab, as an Italian, then in red leather Cossack boots, and finally draped in a Manilla shawl, a carnation behind her ear. A nice little pair, or should I say 'little couple', for there are certain ways and looks that tell their own story and, in addition, the authority assumed by Gitanette, the tender, almost maternal care with which she would wrap a thick woollen scarf round her girl-friend's neck. As for the friend, Nina, Rita, or Lina, I have rather forgotten her. Peroxided hair, light coloured eyes, white teeth, something about her of an appetising but slightly vulgar young washerwoman.

They danced neither very well nor very badly, and their story was that a mass of other "Dance Numbers". Provided they are both young and agile, with a mutual distaste for the *"bar à femmes"* and the *"promenoir"*, then's

the time for them to collect their few pennies together
to pay the ballet-master so much a week to arrange a
special dance routine, and the dressmaker. . . . Then,
if they are very, very lucky, the couple starts on the round
of the various establishments in Paris, the provinces, and
abroad.

Gitanette and her girl-friend were "playing" the
Empyrée that month. For thirty nights running they
bestowed on me all the discreet, disinterested attentions,
the shy, reserved courtesy which seem to thrive exclu-
sively among music-hall people. I would be dabbing on
the last touch of rouge under my eyes when they came up,
lips still trembling from lack of breath and temples moist,
and stopped to smile at me without at first speaking, both
panting like circus ponies. When recovered a little, they
gave me politely, by way of greeting, some brief and useful piece of information: "An eighteen carat audience
tonight!" or else "They're a lousy lot today!"

Then Gitanette, before taking off her clothes, would
unlace her friend's bodice and Nina, or Lina, at once
began to laugh and swear and jabber. "You'll have to
watch your step," she'd shout across to me, "those roller-
skaters have gone and cut the boards to pieces again
tonight, and you'll be darned lucky if you don't come a
cropper!" The voice of Gitanette took up the tale, more
soberly, "It's a sure sign of luck if you fall flat on your
face on the stage. It means you'll come back to the same
place before three years are out. That happened to me at
Les Bouffes in Bordeaux, when I caught my foot in one
of the cuts. . . ."

They lived out loud, quite simply, in the next room to
mine with their door left wide open. They twittered like
busy, affectionate birds, happy to be working together
and to have the shelter of each other's arms and their love

as a protection against the barren life of the prostitute and the occasional tough customer.

My thoughts went back to those old days as Gitanette stood before me, alone and sad, and so changed. . . .

"Sit down a minute, Gitanette, we'll have a coffee together. . . . And . . . where is your friend?"

She shakes her head as she sits down. "We're not together any more, my friend and me. You never heard what happened to me?"

"No, I've heard nothing. Would it be impertinent to ask?"

"Oh, good gracious, no. You see, you're an artiste like me . . . like I was, that is, for at present I'm not even a woman any more."

"Are things as bad as that?"

"Things are bad, if you like to put it that way. It all depends what sort of person you are. I'm by nature the sort who becomes terribly attached, you see. I became terribly attached to Rita, she meant everything to me. It never entered my head that things could change between us. . . . The year it all happened we'd just had a real stroke of luck. We'd hardly finished dancing at the Apollo, when up popped Saloman, our agent, who sent us word that we were to have a dance routine in the Empyrée Revue, a gorgeous revue, twelve hundred costumes, English Girls, everything. For my part, I wasn't so mad keen to dance in it. I've always been a bit afraid of these big shows with so many females in them, for it always leads to rivalries, quarrels, or mischief of some sort. At the end of a fortnight in that Revue, I wanted nothing so much as to be back in the quiet little number we'd been doing before. All the more because little Rita was no longer the same with me; she'd go visiting round here and there, palling up with this girl or that, till it was the bubbly she went for in the dressing-room of Lucie Desrosiers, that great roan mare, who was poisoning herself with the drink and whose stays had all their whale-bones broken. Champagne at twenty-three sous a bottle! Does anyone suppose you can get hold of any decent stuff at that price? The little one was going all lah-di-dah; there was no holding her. Dashed if she doesn't come back to our dressing-room one evening, bragging that the Commère had given her the glad eye! Now I ask you, was that very bright on her part, or very proper to me? I got ever so low spirited and began seeing the bad side in everything. I'd have given I don't know how much for a good date in Hamburg, or at the Winter-garten in Berlin, or almost any place to get us out of the big Revue that seemed never to be going to finish!"

Gitanette turns to look at me with her dark-coffee-coloured eyes, which seem to have lost all their keenness and vitality.

"I'm telling things just as they happened, you know. Don't run away with the idea I've made up this or that detail about anyone, or that there's any malice intended."

"No, of course not, Gitanette."

"That's good to hear. Well, came the day when my little bitch of a pal says to me: 'Listen, Gitanette,' she says, 'I need an underskirt (we still wore underskirts in those days) and a natty one too. I'm ashamed to put on the one I have!' As was only proper, I was the one who kept the key of the cash-box, otherwise where would our meals have come from! I simply said to her: 'Now about this underskirt, it will cost you how much?'—'How much, how much!' she shouts back at me in a rage. 'Why you'd think I hadn't even the right to buy myself an under-skirt!' After a start like that, I saw we were in for a scene.

To cut it short, I just tell her: 'Here's the key, take what you want, but don't forget we've got the monthly rent to pay tomorrow.' She takes out a fifty-franc note, flings on her things helter skelter, and off she rushes, to get to the Galeries Lafayette, supposedly, before the rush hour! Meanwhile I stay behind to run over a couple of costumes just back from the dyers, and I stitch and I stitch, while waiting for her to come back . . . When all of a sudden I see I'll have to replace a whole ninon under-flounce in Rita's dress, and I dash down to the nearest shop in the Place Blanche, it being already dark. . . . Simply telling you the story brings it all back clear as the moment it took place! As I come out of the shop, I only just escape being squashed flat by a taxi that draws into the kerb and comes to a stop, and then what do I see? Lo and behold, before my very eyes, that great Desrosiers getting out of the cab, her hair disshevelled, her dress all undone, and waving goodbye to Rita, to my Rita who is still sitting inside the taxi! I was that taken by surprise, I stood rooted to the spot, cut off at the legs, I couldn't budge. So much so that when I tried to make a sign, to attract Rita's attention, the taxi was already far away, it was taking Rita back to our place in the Rue Constance. . . .

"I'm all in a daze when I get back home; and of course she was already there, Rita, that is. You should have seen the look on her face . . . no, you have to know her as well as I know her, to see what . . .

"There, let's leave it at that! So I act simple and I say to her: 'What about that underskirt of yours?'—'I never bought it.'—'And what about that fifty francs?'—'I lost it.' She fires this off point blank, looking me straight in the eye! Oh, you can't imagine what it was like, you can't imagine. . . ."

Gitanette lowers her eyes and nervously stirs the spoon in her cup.

"You can't imagine what a blow it was to me, when she came out with that. It was like I'd seen the whole thing with my own eyes; their meeting place, the taxi ride, that one's furnished room, the champagne on the night-table, everything, everything."

She goes on repeating under her breath "Everything, everything," till I interrupt her. "And then what did you do?"

"Nothing. I cried my eyes out over dinner, into my mutton and beans. . . . And then, a week later, she left me. *Fortunately* I got so ill that I almost pegged out, for if I hadn't of, though I loved her so much, I'd have killed her. . . ."

She speaks calmly of killing, or of dying, all the time turning her spoon in the cup of cold coffee. This simple girl, who lives so close to nature, knows full well that all that is required to sever the threads of misery is one single act, so easy, hardly an act of violence. A person is dead, just as a person is alive, except that death is a state that can be chosen, whereas a person is not free to choose their own life.

"Did you really want to die, Gitanette?"

"Of course I did. Only I was so ill, you understand, I wasn't able to. And then, later, my granny came to look after me and nurse me through my convalescence. She's an old lady, you see, I didn't dare leave her."

"And now, at the present time, you are less sad than you were?"

"No," Gitanette answers, dropping her voice. "And I don't even want to be less sad. I should be ashamed of myself if I found consolation after loving my friend the way I did. You're sure to tell me, as so many others have told me, 'Do something to take your mind off it. Time is the great healer.' I'll not deny that time does straighten things out in the long run, but there again it all depends on what sort of person you are. You see, I've known nobody but Rita, it just happened that way. I never had a boy-friend, I know nothing about children, I lost my parents when I was quite young, but when I used to see lovers happy together, or parents with little children on their knees, I'd say to myself 'I've got everything they've got, because I've my Rita.' No doubt about it, my life is finished in that respect, nothing can alter it. Each time I go back to my room at Granny's and see my pictures of Rita, the photos of us two in all our numbers, and the little dressing-table we shared, it starts up all over again, the tears come. . . . I cry, I call out to her. . . . It does me no good, but I can't help it. It may sound funny, but . . . I don't believe I'd know what to do with myself if I didn't have my sorrow. It keeps me company."